PERFECT PITCH

Lesbian Feminist Fiction

edited by J. E. Hardy

Published in 1991 by Radical Feminist Lesbian publishers,
Onlywomen Press, Ltd.
38 Mount Pleasant, London WC1X 0AP

Printed and bound in Denmark by Nørhaven.
Typeset in Melior by Columns, Reading, Berkshire, U.K.

Cover illustration copyright © Cathy Felstead; courtesy of New
Woman Magazine.

British Library Cataloguing in Publication Data
Perfect pitch : lesbian feminist fiction.
  I. Hardy, J. E.
  823.0108920664 [FS]
  ISBN 0–906500–41–9

CONTENTS

FOREWORD

J. E. Hardy

edit ('edit) *vb. (tr.)* **1.** to prepare (text) for publication by checking and improving its accuracy, clarity etc. **2.** to be in charge of (a publication esp. a periodical). **3.** to prepare (a film tape, etc.) by rearrangement of a selection of material. **4.** (often foll. by *out*) to remove, as from a manuscript or film (Collin's *Concise English Dictionary*).

If that's what you think I've been doing, you're right. But of all these aspects of editing, it is the selection which is the most daunting task. Each editor will choose for different reasons, be driven by different causes, different concerns, different visions. My editorial instincts led me to select stories on the basis of the skill of the writing, the radiance, the wonder the writers bring to the stories they have written. I was also looking for an essential lesbian feminism under-pinning each author's words.

As I read and chose among the many submissions, I tried to be aware not only of the style and content of each story but also of the over-arching concerns that linked them. The act of writing causes the world to change and this is mirrored in the fluid tapestry of themes found, over time, in anthologies of lesbian feminist fiction. *Perfect Pitch* began as a disparate collection that quickly revealed a tenacious consistency. Many lesbians were writing in similar ways, about similar things: fantasy, journeys, friendships, choices and death. Over and over these styles, these concerns repeated themselves. And so, that is what the reader will find in this anthology: fantastic stories, fables almost, about communities, lovers, frailties, strengths, loss — and, ultimately, our limitless horizons.

There are two bodies of mainstream thought about fantasy writing: that it is essentially negative because it posits worlds that do not exist and is therefore a retreat from the challenges we face; conversely, that it is a positive flight of the imagination, showing what might have been and what might yet be. The latter definition describes what, as an editor, I've tried to create in this anthology. For these writers are not admitting failure, they are not creating other worlds in which to hide. Indeed their worlds are difficult, fraught with dangers. Women and men die in those worlds as they do here. And lesbians make choices.

In Cherry Potts' story, 'Perfect Pitch', Ashe has control over her life and voluntarily forfeits that control. In the days that follow this decision she learns to live with her reduced abilities, overcomes suspicion of women who are not as she is, communicates in new ways. This story/fantasy is many things but the issues of choice and control of our lives are only some of the links between 'Perfect Pitch' and the other stories here. The literary skill of the author and the material details of a lesbian existence we can all recognise ground this story's unspecified period, its characters' unearthly powers, in ways reflected throughout the collection.

'The Visitors' is set firmly in our world and time; the opportunity for change comes from another world. Each earthly woman is offered what she imagines she needs, what each thinks she dreams of, what each sees as her goal: immortality in a lesbian world. Yet once the choice has been so easily offered, it becomes difficult. For, as Alicen says 'To choose is empowering'. Amanda Hayman makes the choice a real,

2

immediate one, a believable one: she offers a chilling explanation of previous massacres of women, and predictions of persecutions yet to come.

'Skin Deep' could be seen as a simple metaphor for coming out, a beautiful, other-wordly image showing the acceptance of women-loving as easy, as something to be welcomed. But there is more than this in Jaq Bayles' story; there is also a call for reappraisal, for change in our real lives, in our expectations. A call to recognise the possibilities, the opportunities around us. My own story, 'Red', mirrors this. Others in the anthology have written fantasies across space, mine is written across time. Red is from another time, across all time. She is free. She has free will and exercises it, wanting Ellen to do the same. Sex without guilt, speech without fear, minds without chains – these are the things she believes and practices.

Both 'The Prickly Witch' by Helen Smith and 'Sulphur' by Lucy Kimbell have fabulist overtones. They are short, moral stories, told with rare, precious economy. The Prickly Witch runs away from the Greedy Girl again and again, but eventually faces the reality of her desires and the true nature of the girl's pursuit. In 'Sulphur' the fable is illustrated with exotic imagery, the story of the knees developing against the background of a comfortable, relaxed relationship, in which the lovers are open to each other, easy with their bodies.

Many of the stories submitted for this anthology told of death, of the loss of someone and the concomitant grief. I will not speculate as to the reasons for this; why so many, why now? Wittgenstein wrote that 'Death is not an event in life'. Charmingly, skillfully, the writers in Perfect Pitch prove him wrong, with ease, again and again. Death is very much an event in life, and the living of the life that remains is hard. The stories speak of rage, fury, misery, humour, of a sense of a continuum, a never-ending lesbian love which transcends these feelings.

In 'A Friend in New England' the grief felt by Helen is for a loss over which she had no control (unlike Ashe in 'Perfect Pitch'). But as she walks the

3

beach, delighting in the things around her, in the simple pleasures of sun and sand, Helen thinks of Lotte, a woman she does not know well, but one of many women to whom she can turn for balm, to anchor herself, a woman who can make Helen feel 'infinitely cherished'. And again we see a woman who is beginning to make choices, who is burgeoning. Maro Green's Ginger feels differently. She is old, tired, in constant pain, furious. She writes a letter to her dying life-long love, a letter stained with retsina and covered in pitta-bread crumbs. A letter in which she describes a journey the two of them never made yet will now always be making, a fantasy crossing land, sea and time. A letter which leads Jean through her dying. 'Any Port in a Storm' is the letter.

Friendships are the focus for many stories here; in 'The Visitors' and 'Friend in New England', and in 'The Innocent Party', 'Member of the Family', 'Second Sight' and 'Valerie's Rib'.

In 'The Innocent Party', Maírín de Barra's dream-like touches vivify and colour the story of Cassie and a nameless narrator, friends who search for, find and lose love. But this is also a story about changes and choice, in which a separation culminates in an ironic confirmation of lesbian community and friendship's connection.

In 'Member of the Family' Cherry Potts suggests the plethora of unsaid things beneath the surface of a quintessentially English event: the visiting of the house and gardens which belonged to a famous novelist and her lover. Ruby, the novelist's sister, watches the different routes the visitors take around the house, routes which demonstrate their reasons for being there; she plays devil's advocate with some, misleads others, shocks nearly all. Aspen's 'Second Sight' is also set in the real world, in real time. And yet it echoes the tone and substance of other stories: unspoken communication between lesbians, the desire to continue, to heal, to live again and again.

Kym Martindale's 'Valerie's Rib' differs from these in describing the change in a relationship from friendship to love. 'There's no protection at all . . .' the climbers repeat over and over. The growth of the relationship between the climbers encapsulates what we all know. As in other stories in *Perfect Pitch*, the writer has created a feeling of open horizons, the vision of overcoming obstacles to arrive where the view is limitless, where people can appear 'sure and moving without hesitation'.

All the stories mentioned so far create a sense of space, of open horizons: in Greece, California, on cliff faces, in woodlands, on beaches, in other worlds, in other times. Caroline Natzler's stories reverse this, seem almost claustrophobic, concerned with the minutiae of life. It is as if the writer has become a conductor of energy, drawing down the possibilities, grounding the sense of the limitless. 'Spring', although it details a drive through the French countryside, ineluctably draws the reader into the car, asks her to feel the atmosphere, see the seat covers, feel them under her fingertips. The picture of Joanne's horizons circumscribed by her parents to the point where she is a silent astute observer is very clear. As the journey plays itself out, the weight of myths, the silence of ages – none of them stated – reinforce the sense of female power and allegiance, highlight male fallibilities. In 'Paths', the weight of unstated, earlier relationships intensifies the acute observation of an oppressive countryside, a narrow-minded populace. But this is a story of an intense – and intensely private – struggle; culminating in an understated, barely apparent but definitely absolute freedom.

There is Hilary Bichovsky's 'The Big Head'. She describes what many of us feel occasionally, what many women will recognise: the desire to be alone, to get away, to 'steal yourself back again'. The paradox of wanting the wide, open spaces, and the loneliness of being there.

These are the stories in *Perfect Pitch*; an anthology I like to think of as charting the flight of a trapeze through a static world, a tracery of narratives, festooned with colour-filled images trailing behind it.

5

PERFECT PITCH

Cherry Potts

Just when it seems I can go on no longer, that my concentration must break, or my voice give out, the song ends. The last notes are carried out across the field on the unearthly wind, to settle on my enemies. I tie them in chords of deathly music, as pure as the ring of hammer on anvil.

I lower my hands, and open my eyes.

I look down on the carnage played out on the field below the rock outcrop where I stand. The hair stands up on my arms as I shudder, and my stomach lurches.

How could I have so lost myself? The complexities of the song I had taken as a challenge to my skill, never thinking of the reality, of the result. I wrap my shaking hands in my skirt.

This then is what I have wrought with two hours of singing:

On the field below there were two armies. Now there is but one. For the payment of a few insignificant gold pieces (a king's ransom, indeed) I, *I* have slaughtered several thousand men and women: holding them helpless whilst those I serve cut them to pieces. I cannot bear to hear them laughing with joy at their easy victory.

How was it I did not realise? How did I not put the two halves of the puzzle together and make a whole?

I look at the people around me and for the first
time see them for the strangers they are. They are
nothing to me. They bought my loyalty, my service.
The price was not high enough to wipe out this
betrayal. This has cost me too high. This has cost lives
I never knew about, nor cared about until this
moment.

I will go home.

I will not look again at the terrible thing I have
wrought, nor at the joy it has caused these erstwhile
allies of mine.

I see it for what it is and will have none of it. I will
not join in their festival making, their celebration.
There is nothing to celebrate in this abomination.
They should be on their knees begging forgiveness of
the goddess for the evil they have caused; as I should,
but cannot. I am corrupt. I can feel the place inside me
that should hold compassion, it is eaten up with
disgust at myself, that I should have sullied myself
with their monstrous design.

When they sing the songs of this day I will not be the
heroine for long. It will be distorted. I will vanish and
it will be a miracle of the goddess, or the prowess of
the warriors on the winning side.

In the enemy camp they will sing of the witch who
destroyed an army with a cruel and evil spell. And
they will not be wrong.

My gift is not for this use. I should not have used it
for such cruelty. How have I become this person I do
not recognise?

I draw away from them, turning myself inward
breathing a short catch of song, watching their mirth
turn to puzzlement then fade into mist. I close my
eyes against the stinging wind.

I focus again on the warped and stained mirror in
my borrowed room. I stare at myself, searching out the
change that must surely show somewhere in my face.

'Fool.'

To have allowed myself to be caught up in the romance of it all: The dashing young king captured in a rash dawn raid; and I was to have a major role in saving him, in destroying once and for all the uprising that has led to this pass. I agreed, eagerly. Who would not? Fame and fortune in one swoop. I persuaded myself it was the right and proper thing to do, never questioning whether the king would know of it, or should be saved, or why an uprising had been necessary in the first place. What was any of that to me?

'Fool.'

My voice echoes, stark and bitter on the cold walls.

I hear a dissonance, and know what has changed, and what must change further: I can no longer trust myself.

I rifle impatiently through my papers with shaking hands until I find what I seek. I smooth the crumpled paper and scan the words quickly, humming the tune to myself. It will serve. I will not wait for doubts to creep in, for questions to unhinge my certainty. Now it must be done. Now, before it is too late and I grow to love what I have become.

I sing.

Changing the last word in each line, 'foe' becomes 'self'.

My voice begins to grate, changed, changing. The last word is barely a whisper. I listen for the echo of Ashe, my true name and there is none.

It is cold, and differing emotions war within me, fear, confusion, grim satisfaction, anticipation, and a desire to laugh.

I will never spin another song, and no one can ever fool me again into murder.

Now there is time to think.

If I would go home I must walk. I stare at the thin slippers on my feet and draw them under my skirt.

I can no longer turn inward and arrive home in

9

seconds. I have no horse and cannot ride. You do not learn to ride if you have no need. My king's ransom might buy a steed but cannot teach me its control. I must walk.

I wrap myself in the warmest of my unsuitable clothes and walk through the deserted halls and out onto the street, holding my gold against my breast, well away from any pickpocket.

News of the victory has reached here, bells ring out and the singing has started. I flinch away from the noise, smiling nervously at the joyous faces about me, trying to hide the fact that I do not rejoice with them.

I find a market stall that is as oblivious to the merrymaking as I and manage to stock my satchel with food, by pointing at what I want and counting on my fingers. The girl is patient in a bored fashion, and stares through me when I find she has shortchanged me and try to explain. She has done it deliberately, and knows I am hardly about to call the town guard. I can afford the loss of the few pennies she has pocketed. I glare at her, and go on my way. I must be gone from here before the army returns, and with it people who will recognise me.

An hour later I am on the east road, heading for home. My feet are sore and the satchel gets heavier with every step. The impetus of unaccustomed fear has gone, leaving me exhausted. The spinning of such a song as this morning's is not lightly carried. I should have rested, I have not yet eaten. My stomach turns at the very thought. I continue walking. The novelty of this form of exercise wears off rapidly as I realise that I don't know where the next village is, or where to spend the night and am unable to ask the few travellers I pass.

I find myself limping, unwilling to put my right foot flat to the ground, so bruised and raw is the sole through the thin shoes I wear. I wonder grimly if I'll still have feet when I arrive.

A shadow falls over me from behind and I move in to

the side of the road to let the horseman pass. He doesn't, he slows to a walk beside me.

'Walking doesn't seem to suit you, lass.' A light amused voice says. I keep walking, my heart sinking as I listen to the idle clatter of his harness. Out of the corner of my eye I can see a bony shaggy horse speckled grey and black, and none too clean about the legs. A patched and dirty trouser leg is stuffed into battered riding boots and a long keen-edged sword bangs gently at his shin.

'I was going to offer you a ride, but if you can't be civil, I'll leave you to walk your feet off in your own company.'

I listen to the intonation, can hear no threat. I wave him on, indicating that I'd be only too pleased if he would pass me by, but he does not go.

'There I was thinking to myself, there's a foolish rich woman in new clothes that are totally unsuitable, going for a stroll in the forest, thinking her money's safe because she's hung it between her breasts. Ah, you're blushing, don't worry, I've no designs on your money, or your body. I thought to myself, I bet she's running away from her husband who beats her. Am I right by the way?'

I shake my head.

'No? Oh well. I think to myself, you should do the sisterly thing and help her out.'

I turn round and stare up into her face, for it is indeed a woman.

'After all', she continues, 'If I'd ever had a husband I'd have run away, but you aren't running away, are you?' Her voice implies disbelief.

I shake my head, I am running away, but not from a husband. She looks as though the only thing she would run from would be someone who had the right to do as he pleased with her. A fair fight would not concern her unduly. She is not unlike her horse; bony, grubby and older than is comfortable for what is expected of her.

Her hair is bound tightly into a plait and is streaked more grey than its original brown, and is crowned with a battered, broad-brimmed leather hat

11

that shades her eyes so that I cannot see their colour.
Her face is long and well creased and lined. Broad
cheekbones are prominent from long hunger and a
hawklike nose divides sharp eyes that are a little too
close together.

She bows awkwardly but with exaggerated courtesy.

'Now that you have inspected me so thoroughly
will you take up my offer?'

I look down, ashamed, and shake my head.

She sighs, and gathers up her reins.

'Where I come from it is at least customary to say
thank you when refusing a good turn.'

I look up again and catch the pained and reproach-
ful look in those sharp eyes, I would not have her
think me ungrateful for her offer. I grab her rein and
she looks down at me. I touch my fingers to my mouth
and shake my head. Unlike the girl on the stall she
does not stare. She frowns in concern and apologises
for misunderstanding and being rude.

'But you can hear?' she asks. I nod. 'Do you sign?'

I shrug, not understanding. She lets go of her reins
again, strips off her gloves. She makes a shape with
her hands then touches the side of her face, then
another sign. I shake my head, and absently admire
the strength in her long fingers.

'That means we are two women alone.'

I see that she offers me communication, and hope
gives a small lurch inside me. I smile up at her and
repeat the gestures, awkwardly. Her hands move
again, I watch closely, trying to make sense of it.

'That means will you ride with me?'

Because she has made the effort to break through
my silence I agree, feeling more secure with her. She
laughs and offers her beautiful hand to help me onto
the horse. I cannot remember the last time I touched
another person's skin.

She tells me to hold on to her belt if I do not want
to fall off. I put my hands through her scuffed and
ragged belt, feel the sword move as I balance its
weight. The horse moves and I stiffen against its
rolling gait, then realise the slowness of it and relax.

'Where are you going?' She laughs at herself, realising that I cannot possibly answer, and changes her question 'Are you continuing east?'

I cautiously unhook one hand from her belt and hold it up where she can see it, in the universal sign of agreement used in the market. She laughs.

'How many days?'

I spread my hand then hold up three fingers.

'Three days, maybe?' Yes, I tell her in my head.

'Walking? You going to the witch city then?' I hold my hand still. There is something about how she says it.

'Do you think they can cure you, is that it?' I sign no: I know they can't cure me.

She shrugs.

'It's your business. Me, I'm going there. Stay with me and old saddlebones, and you'll be there quicker. I'm aiming to get cured, even if you're not. Besides it's not safe for you to wander about on your own without even a weapon, not that you could use one I suppose? I can protect you and cut a day off your journey. And since you're so keen on taking favours, you can pay me with the food that's doubtless in that bag of yours. I've run out of food and money, but brigandry hasn't drawn me far enough in yet.'

Hours later we are in the forest and dark is falling, so she brings the horse to a stop and I struggle to the ground with muscles that will scarcely obey me. The ground beneath my feet is agony, the muscles of my legs feel as though they have been on a rack for several days.

She swings easily from the horse, but once on the ground she is awkward and slow, one leg shorter than the other. I watch her closely as she deals with the horse. A multiple fracture at some point, poorly healed. It must be agony on the horse, and is clearly worse on the ground. I know that no one can heal her. It is too far gone even for mage physic. She has left it too long. When it was first broken, then perhaps something could have been done, but now, nothing. She reaches down a pair of daggers, runs a finger

13

down the length of one, and I know that she made her living as a warrior. I do not want to think of it. I close my eyes against the caress of her hand on steel, my mind wallowing in the gore of this morning. I force it to the more mundane task of searching out firewood. No wonder she is half-starved. An injury such as that would end such a career. What other skills has she?

We prepare a meal together and huddle over the meagre fire. She attacks her share half-cooked and scalding. I worry over her hunger, then my mind drifts to the night ahead. I long for the capacity to set wards and sleep secure, dreading staying awake alone to watch for beasts that normally I could have set on other paths. Or worse, men, who I could once have stopped in their tracks with a snatch of song.

My companion stretches and her joints crack. She walks a slow circle about our camp singing to herself. Her voice is harsh, but she holds the song true, a simple tune, but the words have more significance.

> 'Hold within wheels that spin
> beast knife and man out the spell
> round and round up and down
> cease not your turns now or ever.'

It is clumsy, but it is a true warding song. If I look hard I can see the faint spark of the wheels she has set in motion.

She sits down and I touch her arm, making the only sign I know for what she has just done. It is not a flattering one. She looks taken aback, then laughs.

'No, not me. I learnt that from a witch I travelled with for a while. I don't really know if it works, just superstition. You don't miss much do you?'

I shake my head, confused. She can't see the wards she has set, does not even know that she has set them, whilst I cannot set them, but can see them. I begin to wonder what I have done to myself.

The swordswoman wipes her mouth on the back of her hand and settles into her cloak to sleep.

'You need not fear to rest, lady, I can hear in my sleep. Anything that disturbs us, I can deal with.'

14

I doubt this, but know we are safe within her wards.

'What I don't understand is why you can't sign. You look rich enough to afford the best teachers. Are you only recently dumb?'

I nod. Far more recently than she can imagine.

'Then surely you have connections at court, couldn't you have gone to the witch they hired for the battle instead of traipsing out here?'

I turn my head away so that she will not see the hot flush of shame on my face.

'Squeamish about blood are you? Don't worry, I wasn't there, so I can't upset you with details. They wouldn't hire an old warwound like me even for the childsplay they were at this morning.'

Childsplay. Bitterly I condemn all warriors, and this one in particular. To call a massacre *childsplay.*

I keep my face turned away.

'Goddess.' Her voice is barely a whisper. I turn to look at her and see her eyes gleam in the fading firelight as she stares at me.

'You're one of the rebels aren't you. That's why you were leaving. Running away all right. No wonder you couldn't go to the witch to be healed, she'd have seen right through you.'

I stare at her in astonishment, not even bothering to shake my head in denial. She has woven her two theories of me into such a glorious mess that I can only admire her imagination and at the same time be horrified at where it might lead. She could scarcely be more wrong.

I shake my head slowly and emphatically. She looks doubtful, but shrugs and lies down again.

I stay seated upright, sleep far from my mind, nursing my aches to me as some false consolation for the pain I have caused others, yet I know that punishing myself will not change what I have done. Reluctantly I lie down to sleep, but every time I close my eyes I see that bloody field and all the lives I wiped out. I peer at my hands in the dark, I cannot truly see and imagine them dripping gore. I wipe my palms against my legs.

*   *   *

15

Sleep steals up on me unawares, and when I next open my eyes it is to a feeble dawn and mist hanging from the trees like cobwebs.

The wards flicker faintly and my companion still sleeps. I struggle to my feet and the horse snorts in surprise, she had forgotten me it seems.

The swordswoman does not stir. I smile to myself. So much for her great hearing. I shake her shoulder gently and she rolls suddenly away from me clutching at her great sword but completely unable to get to her feet. She wakes fully and swears at me. Using her sword as a crutch she hauls herself up. She is clearly in pain and I long to be able to ease her. It would only take a few bars of a simple song, and I cannot do it. She staggers bad temperedly away to relieve her bladder and I set about seeing to some food and a warming drink to drive the cold and damp from her limbs.

Now that there is some distance between the town and myself the urgency has left me, and there is only a nagging ache in my mind that tells me to get home and seek counsel of my sisters, and an odd dryness in my throat, that under other circumstances would cause me anxiety, but I need no longer concern myself. A sore throat will never cause me worry again. It is irrelevant. Dimly I begin to realise I must find a new way to make a living, as should my companion. I think idly of getting her to teach me her trade in return for an introduction to those who could teach her mine. But I want no more of killing, although a fair fight with steel is at least honest.

She returns looking less cross, and devours food with no less ferocity than the night before.

She ties my belongings to the saddle and helps me up behind her. I turn to watch her wards fade as we pass them.

Well, if I will not make a warrior, she could certainly make a witch, though her voice is not pure enough for true songspinning. There have been few voices as good as mine for a great many years, and now that number is less by one. I wonder what my sisters will make of me. There will be those who will condemn and those who will pity, and I do not know which is worse.

My companion is whistling to herself; confusion rushes over me. Whistling, surely I can whistle? I can still use tune, it is not the same as song, but there are some small things that do not need words, some small things that can be mine again. I cannot set wards, but I can bring sleep, and take fear. And I can take a little of the pain out of the swordswoman's leg. If I can find the right tune, no words; little damage can be done without words. I have not used my mouth so in years. I am not sure I remember how to control it, I must practise later in secret; I do not want my failure to be witnessed.

The forest seems endless.

Trees: I have never looked at them before, now I look at each and every one, dredging names from my mind. Beech, hawthorn, elder, rowan, oak, elm. Miles of silver birch stretch to each side and above, filtering the light green and strange, peaceful. I long to greet them. My throat aches, and I cough fitfully.

The horsewoman pats my knee carelessly as I lean my head against her back to draw breath.

'If you will travel half-dressed you can expect to catch cold,' she observes. 'Sorcha used to dress like that, but she could keep the cold away.'

Sorcha. I know that name. I know it. Where?

Goddess, yes, I know that name. Surely there cannot be another? Sorcha of the voice like molten sunlight, like iced water? Sorcha who has enough skill for twenty: Sorcha the Songspinner? Can this be the witch this woman once travelled with?

I shake her shoulder.

'What's the matter?'

But I cannot tell her. I can feel tears building up behind my eyes, and I take a deep breath, reach round her and pull at the reins so that the horse stops its weary walking.

'What are you doing?' she asks, astonished. I fall

off the horse, replacing the pain in my thighs for the pain in my feet, and scrabble in the dust. She stares at what I have written, then at me.

'I can't read.' Her voice is small with shame. I stare at her in disbelief, then the tears well up and over and I crouch huddled in the dust and bury my face in my hands, giving myself up to the frustration and anger and grief that has been brewing for a day and night.

She comes to me and tries to comfort me, but I push her arms roughly away and turn my back.

She stands holding the horse at a distance, until I have exhausted myself. I wipe my face on my sleeves and turn and look at her. She hangs her head and plays with the edge of the horse's saddle cloth. She looks up and the anxiety on her face is replaced with a look I don't recognise, but suspect is pity.

'I'm sorry,' she says. I don't know why she is apologising. I hold out my hands to her and she helps me up, brushing the worst of the dust from my clothes.

I try to explain. I make the sign I know for witch and point at her, then again write Sorcha in the dust. I hiss an 'S' at her. It's the best I can do.

'Sorcha?'

I nod eagerly, relieved to have made her understand.

'Sorcha?' Her voice shakes. 'Did you know her?'

Yes, no. How can I explain without telling her who I am? Can I afford to risk it? Hesitantly I shake my head. Her face falls. I catch her hand and make the ugly shape for witch again, then point at myself.

'You? You can't be a witch. You're too young, besides, you've got no voice.' Then her voice stops working and she covers her mouth. Her eyes stare over her hand at me. Black eyes. Bleak and piercing. A tear spills over and trails down her sunken cheek. Now it is my turn to feel guilty and wonder what I have done. She waves me away, gasping. She wipes the tears away angrily, and straightens her shoulders.

'Who did that to you? Who took your voice?' Her voice betrays a deep disgust. She understands what it means. How could she not, having known Sorcha? I

18

shake my head and point again at myself. She stares blankly, not comprehending. I point at myself, touch my lips and shake my head.

'You did it?' I nod. Anger and disbelief light her eyes. She takes off her hat, and drives her fingers into her hair.

'Why?'

I shrug. How could I explain even if I had speech? She sighs, thrusting the hat back on her head. She mounts her horse, helps me up.

I settle on yesterday's bruises and wonder what her silence means. Her back is stiff with anger. She kicks the horse into something approaching speed, which jolts me painfully.

A while later she lets up and reduces speed to the usual awkward rolling walk.

She twists her head round. 'So you're a witch. And you took your own voice. Why didn't you just kill yourself?'

I recoil from the bitterness in her voice. If she wanted she could be a witch, she has such a strong voice. She has the depth of intonation, she has the control. With a little training she could be impressive. Not like Sorcha, not like me. Not a truly powerful voice. But she has the skill. I try to avoid her question, but it persists even though she has turned away to concentrate on the way we travel.

Why didn't I? Because that wasn't the point, I wasn't trying to punish myself. I just wanted to put myself beyond the power to destroy. Destroying myself would have been admitting defeat.

'Sorcha lived for her voice. She couldn't have lived without it,' she says, trying to understand me.

I know of Sorcha's committment, but how does she?

'She would never have given away everything that she was. I hope you got what you wanted in return for your voice.'

Did I? What does she think I wanted? The only thing it was worth, my salvation: and have I gained that?

*   *   *

19

I cannot undo what I have done, but I have made sure I can never do it again. But is that really the answer? I cannot trust myself. If I could trust myself I could have kept my voice. I could still be someone, I could still be myself. I doubt Sorcha ever felt the need to resolve such guilt.

The swordswoman's back is less still. It is difficult to stay angry with someone who cannot argue.

'Sorcha's dead, did you know?' she says in an off-hand, light way that tells me that it is not something she takes lightly.

No, I did not know. I let go of her belt to put a hand to my mouth. I bite hard on my knuckle, trying to drive away the pain by a physical hurt to think on. My eyes sting.

Dead. No one had heard from her for over a year, perhaps even two years. Of course it had been a possibility, but usually you find out. Witches don't die quietly.

Dead. The finest voice in two generations silent for ever, and I cannot sing her a requiem.

The swordswoman stops the horse, and tells me to get off, so I do. She follows me and gets out the food. I do not want it. She shrugs and eats. I want to ask about Sorcha, but I cannot. I want to ask how she came to die, and what she was to this strange woman.

She disappears to walk some of the stiffness out of her legs. I stare at my hands, thinking of Sorcha who sang like a goddess. There are too few of us left. I should never have thrown away my heritage with such haste.

I see again that field covered in bloodied bodies. I shall never be able to wipe that out.

Sorcha. Dead and cold. It takes some believing. I remember the only time I saw her, and I remember her voice. I remember the way the hair lifted on my scalp and her voice cut the air like a finely honed knife; lifting me out of myself. She was like a song herself. I find my throat aching to pour out my tribute to her

20

and the tears well up again. I force them down, force
the ache from my throat, breathe. Then I try, hesitantly,
to whistle. It is ugly at first, then I catch a particular
note that tells me something. I follow where it leads
and there is a tune I do not recognise. A fine tune and
there must be words for it if I but knew them. I falter.
It makes no difference if I know the words. I try again.
Phrase follows phrase and I know that there is
something in the making here. A strong scent of
spinning. I have stumbled on a song of rare power,
and not of my making. It is a song of pain and grief,
and of hope and defiance and love. It begins to wind
down, and then there is silence. I wonder whose song
it is.

I listen to the horse snorting to herself and stamping
one foot impatiently, and to the hurried scrambling
footsteps of the horsewoman. She crashes through the
undergrowth, comes to a halt staring wide-eyed at me,
her hat crushed in one hand.

   'That tune. Sorcha sang that when she was dying.'
   A cold finger runs down my spine. Perhaps I have
paid my tribute to Sorcha after all, and perhaps I have
done more.
   The swordswoman reshapes her hat and thrusts it
back onto her head.
   'You really are a witch.'
   She does not look entirely happy with the thought.
She turns and catches up the trailing reins, playing
thoughtfully with the lead rein, half-turns, as though
to say something further, then mounts and holds out a
peremptory hand to help me up.

As I take her hand a strange sensation takes hold with
her fingers. My pulse speeds up, and my head spins so
that I cannot catch my breath. Dizziness holds me still,
so that she pulls against my resistance. I shake my
head to clear it and scramble up onto the bony back of
the patient horse. I am seeing double.
   I hold on to her belt, and part of me wants to put
my arms around her waist. I find I am sitting more
upright, and that I have finally fathomed the use of my

knees for holding on. I cannot make sense of this, it is as though I have taught myself to ride.

My companion's silence does not trouble me. I listen to the deadened sound of the horse's hooves on leaf mould and dust, and the occasional break of a twig.

Then I realise there is something missing. There is no bird song, no movement of the small animals that have scurried away from us before. The horse's ears turn and the swordswoman slows her. She turns her head to one side then the other, listening, waiting. I feel that there is another presence waiting with us, that if I were to turn my head I would see someone at my shoulder.

Then there is a flurry of movement and we are surrounded by a ring of steel. The horse shies and I clutch at the rider's arm to stay on.

The eyes that stare at us all say the same. A single-minded purpose holds them certain and uncom-promising – knives ready to kill.

For the first time I look death in the face, and wonder if this was the presence behind my left shoulder.

The swordswoman catches my hand to reassure me, a futile attempt.

'What do you want of us?' she asks.

The woman nearest the horse's head catches the reins and replies, 'We want the witch.'

I hear my companion take in her breath, but she does not turn to look at me, to give me away. 'I know of no witch.'

'She sits behind you, woman. We recognise her.'

'This woman is mute, you must be mistaken.'

'She wasn't mute yesterday morning. Enough of this.'

She gestures with the hand that holds the knife, and one of the men grabs my arm and pulls me down from the horse. I fall awkwardly, jarring the arm I put out to save myself. He lets go of me as though I burn him. My head spins and I stagger to my feet, backing away. I am seeing double again, it is almost as if this has happened before.

22

The swordswoman has drawn her long knife. The finest feather touch of hope brushes me, painful in its slightness.She has not forsaken me. But it is pointless against so many and she must know it, even so, the look of determination on her face is equal to theirs.

'I will say it again: The woman is mute. I offered her my protection as we both go in search of a witch to heal us. And I mean to keep my word.'

'You make a habit of keeping company with witches,' another voice says. I cannot see the man, he is the other side of the horse, and my back is to him. Memory supplies a face, but it is not my memory. The swordswoman turns towards him, and her breath escapes in a hiss: a sound of anger and pain. I strain my neck to see her, regardless of the knife a few inches from my face. All I can see is the hand that tightens round the hilt of her knife, knuckles whitening. Such beautiful hands. I notice a small scar just below her middle finger, standing stark and sharp against her skin.

I also see that I can reach her other knife.

I risk a look round to see if they have noticed, but I cannot make my hand obey me, I cannot make it reach up and take the steel.

'Last time we met I took a witch from you, and I shall do it again.'

I watch the muscles tense in her legs and the horse moves suddenly, pulling the reins from the woman's hands, wheeling, front legs flailing. A hand grabs me away and holds me still, as I try to follow her.

It is almost as though a heavy pall of smoke hangs between me and the rider. I see a flash of steel, then there is a scream, too loud to be human. I close my eyes, then resolutely open them again; there is no point hiding from it. The horse staggers, her eyes rolling in fear and pain; blood gushing from her throat, a long choking cry taking her to her death. Her rider throws herself awkwardly out from under the falling body, losing her knife, falling because her legs will not hold her. I strain against the grip that holds me. The woman who first spoke holds a knife to the fallen rider's throat.

23

'We want the witch, not you. We want our blood price.'

Blood price. Then they are survivors of yesterday's carnage. I had not thought there would be survivors. Strangely it comforts me that some escaped.

I tear the bag of gold from around my neck throwing it at her feet. She does not move, I cannot distract her. One of the other women picks it up, weighs it in her hand.

'It that all? Is that all it costs to buy you? Well it is not enough to buy us. We want you as well.'

I feel my throat tightening and find it difficult to breathe.

They close around me, all but the woman standing over the swordswoman, She stares at her then abruptly steps away, wrenching the long sword from her belt, picking up the fallen knife. Her sneer is eloquent.

'Witch lover,' she spits. The swordswoman turns her head to look at me, and I go cold. Her look of total bewilderment and mistrust is like ice in my heart. She has finally realised what I am. And she does not like it. No more do I. I wish I could say anything to take away the hurt in the look she gives me. Then I am hustled away held by each arm and made to run. I stumble, part of me trying to turn, to see what has become of her.

Then there is a great shout, and one of my captors loses his hold on me.

I swing round and see her staggering after us, the knife that had still been in the saddle pack clutched in her hand and a look of terrible hatred in her bleak black eyes. She must be mad: there are seven of them. Why is she doing this?

The man who killed the horse steps back towards her, but is called back by the woman who took the gold. As he turns away from her the swordswoman calls out;

'Come on you bastard, let's see you take another witch from me.'

I see double again. I see a younger version of her, fuller, fresher, whole and sound; a longsword clasped in both hands and the same terrible look on her face.

My lungs fill and a voice rings through the forest.

No Brede, No. It is not my voice, but it comes from my mouth. Fear goes through me like a knife.

She falters, slowing, that look goes from her face and she whispers, 'Sorcha?'

Oh, sweet goddess. No. I am not Sorcha. I am Ashe. I do not want to be Sorcha. She stares at me. I stare back, as uncomprehending as she.

Brede. A wave of warmth and longing shakes me.

Stay back, this is not the way. That voice calls, taking my useless vocal chords and bending them to her will. Then she sings.

A small swift song, and they are all motionless.

My hand reaches out and takes back Brede's weapons, takes back my gold, then throws it on the ground, spilling yellow coin in the dust.

Brede stands as motionless as the others. Another song springs unbidden to my lips. There is crashing in the undergrowth and their horses appear. I mount one with practised skill, and lead another to Brede.

She stares up at me, her eyes full of distrust.

'You are not Sorcha.'

I shake my head. She turns away, limping heavily. She strips her gear from the dead horse, pausing for a moment to caress the bloody neck. She skirts around me to haul herself up onto the horse I offer her.

'What about them?' she asks. I shake my head, a memory of the morning before rising to my mind. I will not allow these to be cut down while I hold them helpless. I set the other horses loose, sending them far away from their riders.

I turn the horse sharply, kicking his sides hard, and leave them all as far behind as I can. Sorcha's song will not hold them long. Brede follows. We ride hard until eventually the horses tire. I slow to a walk and Brede asks, 'What happened?'

Confusion sends her question to the darker reaches of my mind, and Sorcha speaks to me.

Dimly I recognise her, leaning over me her hands gripping mine painfully as she cries aloud her grief. All I can do is try to protect her, it is too late for

25

anything else. Too late for goodbyes or last lingering kisses. I must protect her. I sing. My life goes with every note, as my strength drains away I wrap her in my song. If ever she needs me...

I sway on the horse, unsteady, reeling under the onslaught of Sorcha's thoughts. Brede reaches out her beautiful hand and touches mine. As she does so I feel Sorcha leave me, like a silk scarf falling to the ground, she drifts away, and I have no words for Brede. I squeeze her hand gently, feeling a warmth for her that is more than gratitude for her care. I am myself again. Tired, sore and not entirely in control of the horse I ride.

Brede sighs, tears streaking her face, all her old anguish as new as that day nearly two years before.

'She's gone?' she asks, not daring to hope otherwise.

I nod. That is one thing of which I am certain.

A germ of understanding is left behind in that dark place in my mind that Sorcha inhabited: Brede's need for healing is no more physical than mine, and if I wish it, our healing can be mutual.

I have not let go of her hand. Gently I raise it to my lips. I have no words for what I want to say, but I believe she understands me.

SKIN DEEP

Jaq Bayles

She gripped the sides of the bed with hands clawed by pain, clenching her teeth until she felt her jaw would crack. Anything to deflect the agonising heat which seared her skin. She looked down at her naked body, striped with the sunlight that fought its way through the ragged rips of curtain hanging in the open doorway and she saw that every tiny pore had yielded up a perfect droplet of moisture to sit gleaming on her skin. She watched, fascinated, the flat plane of her stomach and saw the first split appear.

She had come here to escape. It was after the day when she had awoken in tears and found she could not leave her bed. She phoned in sick at work and spent the day in the company of a box of tissues, their cheerful colours mocking her mood. The following day she sat weeping while her doctor told her to take a break. She handed in the note which offered three weeks of freedom from the drudgery of her job and boarded the first available flight. It was thus that she found herself, just three days after that morning of despair, stepping into the dust-dry heat of an Aegean Island. For the whole of the first week she spoke to no-one, only wandered alone through the olive groves; basked in the sun; drank the wine and slept.

Until the woman came.

The woman came one evening and sat at her table.

Spoke to her. Asked her questions she could barely answer with a voice by now so unused to conversation and a mind numbed by a deepening despair she could not understand. At first she was irritated by the intrusion, wanted only to be left alone to watch the reflection of the low moon ride the ripples of the sea. But as she listened to the woman's strong, determined voice, she felt herself uncurling as a cat from a long sleep, her brain stretching and her wit reaching out its claws in sympathy with the yawn of her rousing interest.

When she awoke the following morning in the narrow, wooden bed in the stone cottage, it was with the sound of the woman's laughter in her ears. She thought at first that it was a dream. That the fug in her head from the previous night's retsina was blurring her perception. That as she tumbled into full consciousness the clear, cool sound would translate into the braying of a distant donkey, or the imprecise crowing of a young cockerel strutting the yard next door. But as she opened her sleep-leaded eyes, the features of the woman swam into focus. Her face was creased in a broad smile and she leant over the bed, one hand planted on the mattress either side of her head. And she was talking – tugging at her with her voice:

'Wake up. It's time. We'll miss the best part of the day. . .'

Where were they going, she asked as she dropped her feet onto the stone floor, twisting her body away from the woman's gaze (She wondered, for a moment, why she felt suddenly so shy having lain in the sun day after day wearing only a patch of cotton.)

As she pulled on shorts and a T-shirt her memory of the night returned. She had agreed to walk up to the monastry on the headland before breakfast. Her wristwatch told her it was five-thirty in the morning and she stifled a groan, along with the impulse to fall back into her bed and her dreams. When she turned back to the woman she saw she had understood her shyness and was busy scrutinising the sky.

They walked in silence through air not yet warmed

28

by the sun and she felt her senses sharpen in preparation for the assault that eventual warming would bring: the sharp tang of pine on her tongue, the heady mellow scent of olive, the almost unbearable brightness of orange geranium burning her eyes. She felt herself warm to the presence of this woman who had so suddenly and inexplicably kick-started her back into life.

From a few paces behind she appraised the woman's body in a way she had never dared scrutinise another before. She saw that the legs were powerful – a cyclist's legs with a wide sweep along the outside of the thigh and with diamond-shaped calves, the muscles of which were grooved with a deep cleft running down their length. Her hips were angular and blended into a narrow waist tapering up and out to wide shoulders supporting sinewy brown arms. But it was the woman's hands which held her attention. Long, dark hands webbed with wide veins that flowed up to meet scarred knuckles and slender, short-nailed fingers. The woman wore just one ring – a delicate gold band on the little finger of her left hand. Her face, which turned now towards the sun, was not beautiful, but it was proud, with a solid, square jaw, aquiline nose and high forehead. It would have been unremark-able but for the dancing lights in her pale grey-blue eyes. The woman turned suddenly and caught the scrutiny. She threw back her head and laughed deep in her throat at her own blushes.

'I'm flattered,' she whispered, turning away again.

When they reached the small, whitewashed monastery they sat together on a wall and looked out over the wide sweep of the bay, coming to life now with early morning windsurfers and sun-worshippers. The woman touched her arm and she followed her gaze to a hollow under a grey rock. A snake was shedding its skin.

'Looks painful, doesn't it?' she asked. 'But it's so simple when you think about it. They grow out of something and they shed it. Cast off what they don't need. It's a pity we're not that well equipped.' The woman looked out over the bay again and spun a

29

pebble into the abyss. 'I mean,' she appeared to be speaking to herself now, 'we don't know how to adapt. We carry around the same old skin no matter what. No matter how many changes we go through, how our lives metamorphose, we cling to the same old standards, the same old expectations, the same old safety. The same old skin.'

The woman looked at her and she felt the dancing lights leap deep inside her. She shivered at the sensation. The woman touched her cheek with her long hand and said: 'You should learn to shed.' Then suddenly she was on her feet and running back down the narrow rocky path shouting: 'Last one back buys breakfast.'

They spent the day together – talking, playing backgammon in a bar, lying on the baking sand. All the time the sensation she had felt when the woman looked into her whirled around her body. She recognised it but shut the recognition away. She had only one skin.

That night, as they parted, the woman kissed her lightly on her hand.

Later, she lay on her narrow bed and willed sleep to blanket her feelings. But her body was electric with sensations. She thought of the woman and felt warmth rush between her thighs. Her hand wandered down over her hips as if she had not the ability to control its movements, and in the darkness she allowed the desire she had been denying to take its course.

It was when she awoke to the light breaking in her room that the pain began. The searing heat that leapt over every inch of her skin and left her now looking down at the first split. She should be frantic, terrified, but she felt only fascination and relief as she watched the split widen and join with the others appearing all over her body. The skin peeled back in hair-thin slivers and dropped onto the bed around her. Beneath lay smooth, taut, unlined flesh. A baby's skin, perfect in its honey-coloured hue. She smiled as she stepped out of the old self she had hardly known, and when she saw the woman watching her from the doorway she did not turn her body away.

30

THE INNOCENT PARTY

Maírín de Barra

I miss Cassie. Our friendship was the best. Whenever
I bumped into her, on the street, in the library, at
her door, even if I had seen her within the past hour,
her face cracked into this terrific smile, and she
threw open her arms like meeting me was the greatest
thing ever. She looked like she was trying to embrace
the whole street. There'd be three seconds of
open-mouthed silent surprise, startling to passers-by.
Then she would purr, 'We-e-ll-ll! It's you!' And so it
was.

She was here for three years and in all that time
there was no winter. Our last year was the one with
the insects. One long summer slipped over into a
green Christmas. Spring arrived to find old leaves still
on the trees and immediately it was hot all over again.
People sloped about with the giddy eyes of a lost
night's sleep. Clothes hung loose. Everywhere bronzed
ladybirds dragged their bloated bodies into sand-
wiches and lemonades, into shoes, into dishwater and
sweaty hair. There was always a spider in the bath,
daddy-long-legs over your bed. You saw people trying
to scratch their way out of their bodies as a diversion
to commenting on the weather. It was glorious, pink-
striped, relentless.

Cassie would turn up at my door with a drawled,
'Hi!' and look incongruously coy for the shape she

31

framed in the doorway. 'You wanna go walk by the river?' and off we went.

Down to the canal paths, where we kicked up dust and ate holes into our toes. We sat in the shade, dangling our feet in polluted waters, watching the paint blister on houseboats and wondering at the courage of red bodies huddled over barbeque coals. Mostly we talked. Sorting out the world and asking all the crucial questions. Talked about the heart Cassie had left back in San Francisco, about learning to be wise after the event, about the people we would like to be. Those sort of talks. Or picked greenfly from each other's hair.

When the light began to fade, Cassie would lie back and stare into the sky. She described long drives across North America, slow sunsets on the Prairies. I could see grasslands rolling red and violet before us, and her little orange car a glow-worm out on a long thread. As she spoke, she would gradually cease tugging at the curl behind her ear. I would watch the veins, sharp against her temples, relax, then disappear. The year had been very hard on her.

One night, we went back to her room. Something irritated my nose. I said, 'Jesus! what's that stink?' To be fair, I thought it had drifted in from somewhere else. Cassie stared at me.

'Do you mean my incense?'

'Your incense?' I felt uncomfortable.

'That's right', said Cassie, 'I've been using them to help me meditate.'

I didn't know what she was talking about. I said, with a nervousness I did not recognise, 'Oh! And when did you turn so cosmic?'

Cassie looked at me evenly, went to say something, but just shrugged.

'Are you being serious?' I persisted, incredulous.

'What's the big deal?' said Cassie. 'Just leave it!'

I felt a twinge of shame, but I was bewildered. This wasn't Cassie. I didn't know what to say to her, except a muttered, 'Sorry.'

'Forget it,' said Cassie.

I decided to leave, but Cassie shook her head: 'No. Stay. Sit down.'

32

I sat down awkwardly. Beside me, on a small chest, usually invisible under books, was a neatly ironed green cloth, scattered with gaudy packets. Out of these tumbled smelly sticks and miniature pyramids. I picked up a mustard pyramid, rolled it between my fingers, sniffed it. Looked at Cassie. Then Cassie grinned and flung herself down beside me.

'Hey!' she said, 'before you go, will you try an experiment with me?'

'What kind of experiment?' I was worried in case she had something like ouija boards in mind.

'Nothing like that', she reassured me, 'I just want to see how well I can communicate with you.'

'I've always thought we communicated very well,' I ventured, shrinking from what I knew was going to come next.

'Come on. Just try this,' she urged. 'It won't hurt. Just a bit of telepathy?'

I had a feeling it was going to hurt.

'Think hard.' She had started. 'I'm thinking of a name, a girl's name. You tell me what it is. OK? A girl's name.'

I concentrated.

I could hear her bedside clock ticking away. I wondered what time it was. I didn't want to get back too late. We were going to an all-night dance in London the following day. I had to stock up on sleep in advance.

'Well?'

She was waiting.

'Carol?'

Her lips pursed in disappointment.

'I can't do this!'

'Come on. Let's try again. You just need to relax.'

Relax. I tried to clear my mind. Relax. I heard a voice in my head. It went, 'Clear your mind, clear your mind. Debbie. Deborah. Debs. Make an effort.' Lots of words buzzing round. 'Angela, Moira, Rosemary, Rashida, Roisin, Rusty, Ros, Robert, no that's a boy's name . . . Jen.'

'Well?'

'Oh! Uh . . . Jen?'

That look of disapointment again.

'Are you really trying?'

'I really am. It's just . . . I can't do this. I've tried before. It doesn't work. I'm just not that kind of girl, I guess.' Cassie wouldn't let me give up. 'Maybe names are too complicated for a first attempt. Maybe you are thinking too much. Let's try colours. Just close your eyes and say the first colour that comes to mind. OK?'

'All right.'

I closed my eyes. A colour? I could see a swirling shape that had pink on the outside, with bright green in the middle and lemon in between. It drifted across the plains of my closed eyes and hurt a bit. I realised I had looked at the lightbulb.

I ventured, 'Pink?'

'Yes! See?'

I wasn't so sure. 'I might just have easily have said green or yellow.'

'But you didn't! Let's try again!'

'Why don't we stop while we're on top?'

'No! No. Best of five!'

'All right, but then that's it for tonight, OK?'

'Sure.'

I wanted to please Cassie more than anything. I got the next four wrong.

I couldn't sleep for ages. It was sticky. I lay thinking about Cassie, rationalising the change in her. Maybe it was the heat, stealing off with her sanity. I'm a cynic and a materialist. Cassie knows this. We had always been cynically materialist together. This new revelation about Cassie was disturbing. Made me feel a little bit lonely. Like there was nothing left any more between me, this concrete body, lying on rough sheets, and an eternity stretching everlastingly upwards through the open window. Just a thin ceiling between me and forever, with a few stars to signpost infinity.

When I did sleep, the night made play with my own head. I had one of those dreams you don't want to wake out of and I fought to stay in it as long as I could, then struggled to remember all the pieces. The bits fell together like this:

There were two Chinese women selling satin jewellery cases at a market stall. They were related to the friend that I was searching for. They told me that she was looking for her sick grandmother who had wandered away. I had to go and wait at the house for their return. As I set off, one of the women called me back to show me something. I thought she was going to give me one of the cheap cases from the stall. Instead, she drew out a long, battered box, with corners rounded from wear, and gold paint weathered into streaks. On top, there was an in-laid square of green silk, heavily hand-embroidered. The woman smiled at my pleasure, encouraging me with a nod of her head to take a look inside. The box opened upwards from its base, and a tune started to play. There was no plastic ballerina. Instead, running its length, was a tiny ivory keyboard, each key carved into elongated cats and monkeys and zebras. These moved seemingly of their own accord, worked, I suppose, by some hidden clockwork. The sound was gentle on the ear in a way mechanical music is not.

The woman snapped the box shut and pushed it into my hands.

'Here, this is for your friend,' she said.

I waited in their kitchen for a long time. The grandmother made her own way home. My friend did not come back. I listened to the old woman's stories against the effort of waking. Then they were all gone.

It was only a dream. But it gave me an idea. They do say that in sleep we sift through our dilemmas and weave answers into our less than conscious minds. I decided I would make a box for Cassie modelled on the one the Chinese woman had given me. A peace offering. To hold those damn incense sticks.

We were standing outside, watching women move to a slow reggae beat. Morning was already clashing with the disco lights. A huddle of women leaned on each other, half-dancing, chatting. One of them had a green, stripy t-shirt. My eye followed the stripes round her tummy, imagining my hand was following. 'Definitely cute,' I thought. I watched her bob to the music,

arguing some point to the woman beside her. I
wondered.

Cassie poked me in the ribs and whispered, 'No,
they are not together.'

I said, 'That woman in the striped shirt . . . .'

'is gorgeous!' Cassie finished for me.

'Do you think so?'

'Wow! Yes! Too right!' I think she was teasing me.

At that moment the beautiful one turned to face us,
smiled, said something to one of the others, and
started to walk towards us. It was too easy. She was
going to talk to us. She went straight up to Cassie.

To Cassie. It was unreasonable.

I sustained a distinct stab of anger. Or was it
jealousy? People were always taken by Cassie. I gave
myself a kick. 'Stop it!' I told myself. Meanwhile, I
had missed her opening line. What was she saying?
Something about Cassie being American. They were
wondering if she knew some song or other? If she
wanted to join their band? And could she play any
instruments?

'No, Cassie can't,' I thought, 'And Yes I can, and
Yes, if you are in the band, I want to be too.' But she
didn't ask me. My stomach was having contractions,
like I was going into labour. I wondered if I had
indigestion.

She spoke to me. She said, 'Have you a pen?'

I did. I did. I lent her my pen.

I still felt in a bad mood. Not myself. I think she
asked if I had enjoyed the dance. I think I said, 'No!' I
can be such an enemy to myself. She pulled a face.
Asked Cassie if I always snarled when I talked. I said
something witty, I think. I like to imagine that I did,
anyway. She said something that made me laugh, but
which afterwards I couldn't recall. Thinking back, I
could remember only that her eyes were golden, and
shiny, and very long. When she smiled, her eyelashes
crushed up against her lids. One other thing I
remember: when she was talking to us, she had rested
against me as though I were an old friend. She had
written her name as Sira.

I threw myself into making Cassie's present. I shopped

very carefully to find wood that I could recycle. Found some heavy green satin and stocked up with silk threads. I was determined that, as far as possible, it would be just like my dream. I played it out like it was an omen. I can bang in a neat nail and have the tools to carve. But I couldn't even attempt to make the keyboard. I had to think of something else. I decided that my box would open into a row of engraved Chinese paint sticks. There was a shop in town that sold charcoal blocks, decorated with stock-in-trade blue mountains, elaborately twisted green trees and startling white waterfalls. You were meant to crush these and blend them with water, but it was hard to imagine that anyone ever did.

For a week, I hardly surfaced. It became an obsession, but it was not the only thing on my mind. When I planed down the wood, I thought of Sira, and the heat of her arm against mine. I imagined her eyes looking back at me from the polished wood. Her laugh ran through my head until it faded into my own. When my thoughts of her were exhausted I rang Cassie, asking for reinforcements.

'When she came over to us at the disco,' I would ask, 'what was it she said first?'

'Oh, I don't know,' said Cassie, 'Nothing earth-shattering, as I remember.'

'Well, when she was talking to you, was she looking over at me?'

'No, she wasn't,' Cassie protested.

'But, you do think she's nice?' I would persist.

'She seems quite pleasant,' Cassie would reply.

'Maybe, we could arrange to meet up, seeing you have her address?'

I had lots of ideas about the way Cassie could help me through this one:

'You could ring her up, Cass, and ask her down for the weekend. Then maybe you would have to go off for several hours because of a previous engagement. And I would kindly oblige you ... Then maybe we could suggest that, as there is more room in my house than yours, she could stop over here for the night. As she was too tired to travel back.'

'If she was too tried to travel back,' said Cassie.

'We could tire her out.'

'Well, maybe. I'll think about it.'

It didn't happen. I began to wear out my memories. Except those golden-brown eyes would glance back at me off shiny objects, or from glass doors in telephone booths, or off the taps when I brushed my teeth, or as squashed up reflections in car windows. One day, I asked Cassie again if we could arrange to meet up with Sira. She looked annoyed, and snapped, 'Has your needle stuck?' So I dropped the subject.

I took the box round to Cassie's. I told her that I had made it myself.

'So that's what happened to you,' she said.

I knelt to fill the box with her incense bits, while she watched me, pulling on the curl behind her ear, one eyebrow raised. Mission accomplished, I handed it over. Her expression held a hint of suspicion, but she took it from me and inspected it from all sides. 'It's very nice.' Then she added, 'Really.'

'You do want it?' I asked. I wasn't sure.

'I've never seen anything like it,' she replied, 'It's very special.' She sat down on the floor beside her bed. Opened the box. One by one she took out the paint sticks and laid them in a row along the table. Then she closed the box, placed it on her knee and took hold of my hand. We sat like that.

A few weeks later, I was sitting in my room working, sweating. Cassie had gone to London 'to see to some business'. I couldn't concentrate. I wanted to know what she was doing. I wouldn't ask. It had entered my mind that she was going to meet Sira. It was irrational. Why would she do that without telling me? She wouldn't. Occasions like these make me wonder what kind of warped personality I have. How could I place such little trust in her? My best friend? It didn't make sense to think like this. Still, I felt I knew where she was.

I had to talk to her. It was late; she would be back. I

phoned. She wasn't home. An hour until the next train from London. Go to bed and forget it. Sleep.

Two hours later, I got up and phoned again. No, she wasn't back. A tired flatmate yawned into the phone that maybe I would like to try tomorrow?

At half-past seven in the morning I was on the telephone. Shocking. What was this behavoiur of mine? The equivalent of men checking up on their wives the minute they went out of the door. I didn't know what I wanted to say to Cassie when she answered, much less how I could explain ringing her at that time in the morning. They said she wasn't in.

She didn't come back for two days.

When I met Cassie in the street, I went straight onto the attack.

'You saw her, didn't you?'

'Saw whom?' she said, with a feigned look of boredom.

'Whom? Whom? You know very well who!'

Cassie shrugged and went to walk on.

Was that all she was going to say? After all, she could tell me I was wrong. I caught up with her. 'Well, did you?'

She stopped walking. Turned to face me. Put her hand on her hip. Made out like she was chewing gum. All intended to underline how pathetic I was.

'Yes, I did.'

'And?'

'And what?'

'Well, what happened?'

'What happened?'

'Yes, what happened?'

'That, I believe, is my business.'

And so it was. Her business.

It was her business but it seemed to me it was my business too. We had let someone come between us. If that wasn't bad enough, I still wanted to see Sira but it now seemed an impossibility. I didn't know how to contact her except through Cassie. And I didn't know what Cassie was thinking. Sira's name hung unspoken

39

between us. I took refuge in blaming things: the heat, mosquitoes, our constricted lives, Cassie's rough year. I resented Cassie for her silence, for sneaking Sira from under my nose, for risking our friendship. Then I wondered if our friendship had been the real risk and her behaviour the symptom. Futile thoughts.

We still met up, Cassie and I. Cassie used to grin when she saw me, spread her arms out as though she was going to catch the earth, then drop them swinging at her side, like she had just missed.

'So,' she would say, 'shall we go some place? I have shopping to do.'

Then we might bustle through half-deserted streets, over bleached white tarmac, busy together. Sometimes, on our twilight walks beside the river, we sat up close, arms wrapped twice around, or pressed our scalps hard against each other like old times.

Our talk, now, was of the 'whens' rather than the 'ifs' of her return to the States. She was very unhappy. I still wanted to make things right for her in a way that just was not for me to do. She said she would never come back to England. Had to find a place where she could leave and come back without, each time, having to argue her legitimacy with racist Customs. She asked me to consider coming to California instead. California was not a real place to me. She said she would miss my friendship. I said, 'Me too.' I was missing her already.

I helped Cassie to leave. I went round to help her pack the books she was mailing home. I sat on the bed, struggling to find the end of the sellotape. She said, 'There's a scissors about, somewhere.' I rooted around on the little chest, looking under the stacks of papers and cards and chocolate wrappers that had accumulated. I saw the bright blue and pink packaging of some jasmine sticks. I picked them up, turning the packet over slowly as though I knew I had to do something with it but I wasn't quite sure what. Then I shook myself. Of course. I could put them into the green-topped box. I pushed the papers out of the way to find it. Them I moved everything off the chest and replaced them one by one. It wasn't there. I glanced round the room. Everywhere there were piles of books and clothes ready to be packed.

'Cassie?' I called.

She popped her head around the door. 'Yep?'

'I wanted to put these sticks away. Where is that box I made for them?'

'I haven't got that any more.'

'What?'

'I said, I don't have it any more.'

Nothing would induce her to say anything else about it. I didn't know whether I should be feeling sorry that something had happened to it, or angry that she had not taken more care of it. I argued with her, told her how much I had put into making something special for her, that I had a right to some answers.

Cassie said, 'Did you make it for me or for you? I thought you gave it to me.'

Maybe she was right but it seemed very hard. I was upset, angry. We argued, me insisting on knowing, she refusing to be pressurised. Eventually, she gave me one of her looks, and told me to go home if I felt like that. She didn't want a hard time over it.

That was my limit. I stalked out in a sullen silence. She didn't call me back although I closed the door slowly in case she did. I considered phoning her, but had nothing new to say. I hoped I would find one of her punchy notes stuck under my door. None came. She didn't try to contact me as far as I know. Left no forwarding address nor any of the things she had said she wanted me to have when she went home. I didn't even have her photograph. I felt bitter.

That was two years ago and I thought there had been an ending. On Tuesday I went for a drink with Trina, a woman from the office, who, by chance, met an old friend of hers at the bar. She brought her over to join us. It was Sira – who gave me a brilliant smile and said 'pleased to meet you', as though we had never met before. She didn't recognise me. Not a hint. I was stunned. Mortified, even. What was this? After the months I had spent brooding about her? After the trouble she had wreaked between Cassie and myself? Surely my face was engraved into her consciousness, etched into her psyche, burnt into her soul? Apparently not.

There was, however, some compensation. Sira smiled into my eyes while she quizzed me in small talk, watched my lips while I talked. Her palm was warm on my arm, on my thigh, while she followed my brain working. Gratifyingly smitten. Both of us. I dedided not to mention our first meeting.

And so, maybe it is coming to be as I had always thought it should be – it. Romance, that is. Sira and me. Women afloat. Tip-toeing on air. All that stuff that makes my cheeks hot. The intricacies of this great love story that is bound to be ours.

On Thursday night, we went back to Sira's flat. She has very Spartan taste in decor. Lots of clear spaces, empty walls, and unpatterned fabrics. She says she does not like complication in her life. One or two photographs and a striped bedspread suffice for ornamentation. Thursday was a very cold, clean night. Sira was teasing me for moaning about my frozen toes. 'Cold nights like these are wonderful,' she said. 'The earth's heat is going straight up into the atmosphere precisely because there are no clouds. That means you can see all kinds of things in the sky. Look!'

She pulled back the curtains to show me, and started to point out configurations of stars. She has a very scientific mind.

I didn't see the sky. Behind the curtain, a solitary object graced the window-ledge, and that was the box I had made for Cassie.

I put my hand to touch the satin top.

Sira saw me, and said, 'Oh, do you like that?' She picked it up to hand it to me. My hands froze in mid air so that I could not take it from her. 'It opens this way, unusual isn't it?' She opened it. 'See? Like that? It's very handy because it means I can keep this inside.'

She lifted out what looked like a small glockenspiel made out of ivory. Each bar was carved in the shape of an elephant. 'It really works,' she said. 'My grandfather made it for me years ago. He was a sailor who jumped off a French ship to live in China. He's dead now.'

'Where did you get the box?' I asked.

'Oh that? It was a present. The year before last, I met an American woman. She came down to hear our band play and we thought it would be fun to show her the sights of London before she went home. We organised the whole tourist thing for her, you know, the Tower, and the Jewels, and Brixton market. A bit of everything thrown in. I've lived here all my life and never seen them myself. I put her up here for the night. It was so hot. I don't know if you can remember that summer? I opened up the windows to let in some air. She saw my glockenspiel there and started to play . . . what was it she played? "Swing Low, Sweet Chariot." That was it.'

Sira took one of the batons that lay in the box, and started to pick out the tune, humming to her own accompaniment. It was just as I had heard it before. When she had run through the tune once or twice, she put the baton back into the box, and laid the instrument on top. I waited for her to continue.

'After she had finished playing, she went to her bag and took out this box. She said it was very special to her but she wanted me to have it. I didn't want to take it.'

'But you did,' I said.

'Not exactly.' Sira traced with her finger the outline of a young girl I had carved into the wood. 'I thought she meant it as a thank-you present, for showing her around, looking after her. I told her I would be just as happy with a post-card from the States, with her address so that I could write to her. She said it was nothing to do with that. It had to do with a friend of hers. And the glockenspiel. That they all belonged together. Rather quaint, isn't it? I didn't understand, but this box is great.'

Sira held the two objects up side by side. 'See? A perfect match.'

Then she added, 'I did, for one moment, consider

giving her the glockenspiel. It would have been hard to part with it but it seemed mean not to give her something in return. I thought about it, but it didn't seem the right thing to do.'

After a pause, Sira said, 'The woman, Cassie, put the glockenspiel inside the box, closed it, and pressed it into my two hands. She said, "Anyway, this was meant for you."

I think maybe she was a bit mad.'

A FRIEND IN NEW ENGLAND

Lis Whitelaw

The beach gleamed in the morning light. 'We just don't have beaches like this in England,' thought Helen as she scuffled through the loose, warm sand of the dunes on her way down to the seemingly endless expanse made firm and solid by the tide. Once there she paused, digging her toes deeply into the cool, hard sand. The bay curved away from her, a smooth arc stretching to where sky and sea merged in a hazy distance. The sand was white, the sky blue and the ocean the blue-green of Venetian glass. 'Really the way they are supposed to look,' Helen thought and the recognition made her absurdly happy. This was what a walk on the beach was meant to feel like; it was meant to be a treat.

She set off down the beach, away from the hot-dog stands and surf-board rental, away from the densest throng of people, the people who could not bear to be more than feet away from the car-park, the ice-cream seller or the showers. She planned to walk as far as the first group of houses, grey, wooden and right on the beach; houses where she had once dreamed of spending the winter looking out at the Atlantic. At the moment they were made slightly indistinct by the haze and the distance, but she knew every detail of the carving on their verandahs – how some had plain slatted rails while others had elaborate barley–sugar twists. How some had porches with columns and carved lintels, while one house, her favourite, had the weather-boarding arranged in a sunburst over the blue-painted front door.

With this as her goal, Helen walked down the beach to the edge of the water. The sea was shallow, far too shallow for swimming and it remained at this depth for some twenty yards, stretching out to where the surf broke in a steady line of foam and noise. The water was icy cold against the sun-warmed skin of her legs but after the initial shock Helen enjoyed the contrast of sensations, revelling in the pleasure that such simple things could give her once again. As she walked, she played her favourite game of watching people and telling herself stories about them.

This was a good place for such games because her fellow walkers divided themselves into several clearly defined categories. Here on the Maine coast there were always large numbers of French Canadians, either visiting from Canada, or just as likely, from other parts of the state where they worked in the remains of the textile and footwear industries. So the first game was to decide whether or not, when she walked past them, they would be speaking that version of French which she found so completely incomprehensible. After a while Helen found that there were certain tell-tale signs, the most reliable of which was the style of their bathing suits. French Canadian women were those with the highest-cut legs and the deepest cleavage – very often in black or brilliant pinks and yellows. One girl, long-legged and deeply tanned, jumped the waves with her friends like a child. Immediately noticeable in a pink bathing costume she had already crossed the frontier into womanhood while her companions, skinny or lumpy in striped bikinis, had not yet caught up – but none of them had noticed. The men wore the briefest trunks and both sexes played ball games, self-consciously, arranging their movements carefully for maximum effect. Helen thought how European this made the beach feel; it reminded her of all those Frenchmen who insisted on playing volley-ball on

46

Mediterranean beaches even though there was less than a hand's-breadth between the basking bodies, and of the way they watched the women watching them.

She gradually found, however, that there was another group which wore minute swimming costumes and played energetic games with wooden racquets and hard rubber balls. She noticed one young man, broad-shouldered, well-muscled and tanned and two young women watching him with unembarrassed pleasure, admiring what was clearly to them an ideal male body. He was one of a group of men, some of whom were already stretched out in the shade of umbrellas. When he bent to kiss one of the sunbathers the young women turned silently away. After that incident Helen realised how many groups of men were walking together, less protective of the space around them, more ready to touch than usual. As so often she found it much harder to identify which of the all-female groups were made up of lesbians.

Helen realised that today she was looking more intently, paying real attention to the people who passed her. They contributed to her sense of elation, of almost limitless energy, filling her with delight at being surrounded by people who were so evidently enjoying themselves. A woman, probably in her early seventies walked by, deep in conversation with a man. She was dressed in a black t-shirt and khaki shorts and, rather unexpectedly, her grey hair was covered by a beige baseball cap. The cap was completely plain, without any of the usual badges proclaiming support for a sports team or a manufacturer of trucks or agricultural machinery. Its plainness caught Helen's eye, surprised her, made her notice the woman and in noticing become aware of how stylish she looked, even though she was wearing the same uniform as nearly everyone else on the beach. Once she had noticed one older woman Helen became aware of how many there were, walking alone, in groups with other women, with men. Confident, relaxed women, at home in their bodies; no longer minding that their thighs sagged or that the sun emphasised the lines on their faces and throats. Unlike the younger women they were able to give their complete attention to their companions; unconcerned about the effect they were having on the world at large they were able to enjoy the pleasures of the morning as simply as the small children who ran screaming in and out of the water, screaming for the sheer joy of being alive, here and now on miles of sand with the ocean to play in and parents and friends to play with.

Helen passed a group of sandpipers scuttling along the beach, their legs moving rapidly as though driven by clockwork, flicking in and out among the groups of walkers and sunbathers. She thought how odd it was that they showed no fear of people and noticed with surprise how white the feathers of their underparts were.

She enjoyed the assurance, the apparent contentment of the older women but inevitably such reflections forced upward the memory which had been hovering below the surface of all this bright, sparkling excitement – the remembered pain that she had been waiting for, knowing that eventually she would begin to think about last year. Unable to walk and think properly at the same time she sat down in the warm sand at the edge of the dunes.

It was certainly the same beach but in every other way it was entirely different. Then, the damp, grey mosquito-laden weather had kept her indoors for days, until, desperate at her confinement, she had driven off to this then-unknown strip of coast. The tide had been out, just like it was today, but then the beach had been nearly deserted as sea-fog swirled in a ragged breeze and the surf pounded on the bar. Occasionally the wind had blown the fog far enough away for a chill, silver sun to appear briefly in a patch of pale blue sky before it again became obscured by the wandering clouds. Alone in that grey, cheerless world her isolation had felt complete. As so often, fragments of poetry and prose had drifted through her mind: 'No man is an island', 'Its melancholy, long, withdrawing roar' and she had wept for all the people in her life whom she had lost, but mostly she had wept for Maria. Over and over she had thought, 'There's nothing

48

now between here and England, just empty ocean.' For some reason the thought had seemed impossibly sad.

And yet it had been to that same ocean that she had turned for comfort one day soon after Maria's death. Then, still dazed with grief, she had driven to the coast and walked on wide silver sands in the tentative sunshine of an English April afternoon. She had never understood the impulse, but when the friend who had come to keep her company had asked what she wanted to do, where she wanted to go on the first occasion that she had left the house in three days, she had said, 'To the sea, to walk on the beach.'

In the first few months she had immersed herself in the kind of activities that Maria had shared with her – attempting, in what she later came to recognise was an increasingly desperate way, to expiate her guilt for all the times she had resisted going to an opera or a cinema. Without Maria she had done all the things she had so often refused to do with her until she had finally realised what she was doing and brought an end to these ordeals of self-recrimination and disappointment.

Last year's trip to America had been a chance for Helen to enjoy something totally unconnected with Maria. Maria had never been to America. Somewhere deep down she had distrusted its energy which she saw as uncivilised, even dangerous. Helen had been free to take from it whatever it offered; whatever she needed.

And it had offered Lotte. Lotte, who at that moment was probably sitting on her terrace ten miles away or moving slowly round her garden to choose the flowers to decorate the lunch table which she and Helen would share in a few hours' time.

When Helen had mentioned that she was coming to Maine, a friend's mother had said, 'You must go and see my old friend Lotte. I'll never get to see her now but I'd love to know how she is. I think you'd like her.' Deeply distrustful of such prophecies and unsure of her ability to cope with meeting new people, Helen had delayed writing to Lotte until the last possible moment and had then been disconcerted to receive an

49

invitation to lunch. 'I work in the morning and sleep in the afternoon,' the card had said 'but since you're here such a short time you'd better come to lunch.'

Helen had accepted, but the tone of the card and her reluctance to meet her evidently rather grudging hostess meant that she had arrived at the white weatherboard house tense and dry-mouthed with anxiety. Like so many New England houses it defied the brutality of the winters with Puritan determination and sat on a piece of rising ground looking out over the bay, apparently unprotected from the Atlantic gales. Yet somehow Lotte had managed to surround it with an English garden of herbaceous borders and rose-bushes – the only visible sign that many years ago she had left a whole way of life to settle alone on this rocky outcrop.

Tall and grey-haired, Lotte had made no concessions to entertaining. She was dressed in worn jeans and a flannel shirt, both of which hung loosely on her bony frame. 'My gardening clothes,' she had said by way of off-hand explanation. Helen, who had changed out of t-shirt and shorts, immediately felt overdressed. At first she had found it almost impossible to talk to Lotte. Then, during the initial exchange of information about themselves and their mutual friend, she had spilt her sherry and, in the confusion of apology and reassurance which followed, her anxiety and stiffness had vanished. They had not talked in detail about their lives, had not become intimate, but when Helen left two hours later she felt better than she had for months.

Lotte had no idea that her existence was so important to Helen and Helen knew that she would never tell her. She drew strength from Lotte in a way that she did not from people on whom she could make demands in more conventional ways, asking them for help with the garden or simply for company on a particularly lonely evening. Many times during the past year she had tried to analyse what it was about Lotte that she found so nourishing, so sustaining. Why, when the older woman had unexpectedly hugged her goodbye and growled, 'You take good care

50

of yourself, girl, you hear,' she had felt so infinitely cherished.

True, Lotte was the most recent in a line of women who stretched back through Helen's life. Most of them had done nothing in particular, had simply been there, more or less often, more or less continuously. Once Maria had crossed over into a different kind of relationship. Helen knew that if, when she returned to her hotel, there was a message to tell her that Lotte had cancelled their lunch appointment, she would be disappointed but that it would change nothing. If she never saw Lotte again she would still be able to draw on her presence among her flowers and her pictures. One flash of empathy had made the connection.

She sprang to her feet and began to walk up the beach again. 'I'm not going to get as far as the houses now,' she thought. And then she spotted a perfect landmark to aim for. High overhead, bucking and twisting in the breeze, was a kite shaped like a slice of water melon. A wedge-shaped semi-circle, its green rim and pink centre looked so juicy and edible that Helen laughed aloud. The wind caught her voice and tossed it in the air as she shouted with delight, and, unable to stop herself, ran, for the sheer joy of running, along the beach.

SPRING

Caroline Natzler

The poplar trees shivered, wan. It was spring.

As the three of them drove, they heard in the air pigeon noises light as cuckoo song. The fields lay combed, an edge of wind scything the green, and vines squatted along lines of sticks like grave posts in bare earth, under a grey sky. There were no people.

'Do you mind if we shut the window, dear?' Mrs Langley's hands fluttered over her stockinged knees.

Mr Langley frowned slightly and pressed a button on the dashboard so that the window on his wife's side slid up.

In the back Joanna, who was nine, sucked a yellow car sweet she didn't really want, because there was nothing else to do. The seat beside her was empty.

They whirred through hamlets of stone walls, the outer walls of farm courtyards huddled together for comfort, barren but for shaky clusters of wisteria. They saw no people in the villages either, though sometimes a tractor grumbled in the distance.

'Where are we going, Daddy?' Joanna's voice was flat.

'Chateau Grandcourt. Fifteenth-century, a magnificent fireplace, the largest collection of armour in France, a fine formal garden, and a special lunch for little girls who don't complain.' Her father beamed at her in the windscreen mirror.

Joanna put her mouth to the window. She breathed slowly on the glass and watched the shape shift and settle into a ghostly face, and vanish.

They passed a scratched-out farmyard with an old gate like a loose tooth.

'Are we – are you sure we're on the right road, dear?' said Mrs Langley as they crossed a stony white track and the road narrowed and became rougher.

Mr Langley accelerated.

'Rosalind, I think I know this country better than you. I didn't spend five years of my life here for nothing. Besides . . . I want to drive through Pont du Sec.'

Mrs Langley flushed and turned her wedding ring.

'Just historical interest, old girl!' Mr Langley laughed, sweetly. 'The silly girl must have been married the last fifteen years – probably some old hag swathed in black by now.'

Mrs Langley touched her blonde hair carefully and turned a full smile on her husband. 'I know, darling,' she said softly and looked round at Joanna. 'All right, sweetie?'

Joanna nodded and stuck another sweet in her mouth.

If Michael was there, Joanna thought, his face would have sprouted into a grotesque kiss behind their parents' back, his eyes rolling, and they could have giggled together and everything would flow again. She looked at the shaking tops of the poplar trees, in thin copses at the back of the fields, each leaf shivering separately. An old woman opened a gate and Joanna heard her clucking at her chickens, then she was gone.

One holiday they'd had in France, before Michael went away, he'd tied a headscarf solemnly under his chin leaving a tumble of fair hair loose on his forehead, and they'd gabbled together for hours in pretend French, like two old women they'd seen in a market arguing over a fish; they'd roared and gesticulated and ended up tickling and slapping each other with pretend fish and pretend live chickens. But that was all babyish of course, thought Joanna.

The back seat seemed long and hollow and her parents' seats reared up in front of her, the thin lines of the material dizzying to the eye. And the car drummed on to some place she couldn't care less about, though it seemed to be making her mother twitchy.

If Michael was there, she thought, they could just get on discussing something, spinning wordy inventions as long as they could hold out, till Michael's accounts burst impossibly wild and silly and they'd simply dissolve, tumbling into each other until their parents told them to stop. Joanna laughed warm for a moment inside.

Anyway Michael wasn't there. Since he'd been at boarding school he'd been off on his own holidays with bullet-headed friends in grey shorts who went shooting with their fathers in Scotland and thought they knew it all.

One stiff step after another now. The house was glum and Joanna did her homework alone up in her room most evenings. At school there were popular girls who flashed their popularity around and used nicknames and the others, whingey or stupid, who somehow got in Joanna's space, so she wanted to hit them. She didn't mind the quiet new girl with brown hair and odd, still eyes. Her hands were hot when Joanna partnered her in gym once. But she hadn't talked to her much. She didn't really have friends, which she hadn't noticed when Michael was at home; they knew what other people were like and got on with things together. But now, Joanna thought, scratching her wrist vaguely . . . had he really gone over to the other side?

Her chest ached. She breathed warm on the glass again, tucking the sweet under her tongue, but the mist pattern vanished almost instantly and she thumped the seat next to her.

'What is it?' Her mother flicked round.

'Why did Michael have to go to boarding school? Why couldnt I go?'

'You're a girl, darling,' said her mother, surprised. 'Boarding school isn't the right place for girls.' She sighed. 'Michael will be home for the last week of the holidays – and then we'll have him all summer too.' Her eyes were watery.

Joanna thought how her mother had put on her distant, noble face the weeks before Michael went, only her chin wobbling tearfully at times. But he had to go.

Joanna stuffed two more sweets into her mouth. They didn't fill her.

The sky was thin, slivers of white and grey clouds skimming the hollowness. Rain streaked across the windows. Mr Langley sat silent, pressing on large and solid through the shivering day. His daughter reached forward and stroked his soft fair hair, cropped short as hay stubble above his neck, the same colour as Michael's. Mrs Langley smiled fondly at her husband and daughter, and edged her hand up to his on the steering wheel.

'Have a look at the map, will you Rosalind dear,' he said.

Mrs Langley bit her lip and shuffled with the concertina pages of the map.

'All right, I'll do it.' He stopped the car abruptly so that little stones were flung up from the wheels.

The trees edging the road creaked in the wind. The car was thick with silence as Mr Langley concentrated on the map. A blur of blue condensed out of the rain, an elderly man walking slowly towards them. Mr Langley scowled at the map. The man came closer. His face was knotted and closed but he glanced at them with lizard eyes from under his cap.

'You could ask the man?' said Mrs Langley.

Mr Langley immediately started the car, spattering the old man with water as the wheels skidded.

'It's just round the corner!' he said cheerfully.

'Pont du Sec?' murmured Mrs Langley.

Mr Langley shoved up the gear stick and nodded.

The air in the car was tight. Wet fields and trees smeared the windows as they drove on, getting nearer.

Joanna's nipples hurt, pricking. Once Michael had told her, blushing, 'I used to think my nipples were my feelings. I thought that's what hurting my feelings

55

meant.' 'Pathetic,' she'd shrugged, instead of hugging him. But she'd hugged him when he was little and frightened of snakes at the bottom of his bed, and she'd peeled the bedclothes off and shown him there was only his curled-up toes.

That must have been ages ago, she thought. She drew her hair dark and warm across her mouth.

When Michael had got on the train to go to boarding school for the first time, with the other scuffling, noisy grey boys, he'd leant out of the window holding Teddy Jim by the arm and thrust him at their mother. 'I don't want this,' he said, white, and sat down behind the glass.

'But you're allowed teddies the first term,' she pleaded, nursing the bear. Two other boys were craning at the window, shouting something.

A low-walled cemetery with grey tombs like roof tops edged the road. They came to a small town. Mr Langley slowed, pursing his lips, but the sign said Villeneuve, and they sped on through the wan streets, umbrellas and people scurrying in and out of shops with their heads down.

Joanna watched, sucking. Boys had milled on the gravel outside Michael's school, weaving around in their duffle coats, which they wore slung by the hoods like cloaks so they had to keep their heads down. Michael had shown Joanna and their parents round the classrooms and chapel, waxed corridors and desks of rotting wood. He chatted on about boys called Harris Maximus and Smith Minimus and important rules. Boys with large scuffed shoes slid bored looks at Joanna and dodged past, and there was a warm smell, rather sour, which seemed to come from inside bodies, walling her out.

In the open countryside again the rain drifted away, evaporating in sunlight which blanched the vineyard sticks and occasionally flashed into the car. Mr Langley put on his dark glasses and lowered the window slightly. The poplars flickered, pale undersides gleaming like fleeting fish. In the next village they passed three women on their knees, scrubbing clothes at a low water trough beside red and blue buckets bright as tulips.

'Look at those old gossips, right out of a Fragonard!' snorted Mr Langley. 'More French homes have a TV than a domestic water supply. And it's because there's no demand.'

Joanna thought how when she saw Michael now he rattled with things he knew – square roots, economic policies, physics, the right way to pronounce the 'v' in Latin – and smirked when she could no longer argue and tried to find business of her own to slip away to. 'Ignoramus, cretin . . .' he shrugged, so that once, fizzing inside, she'd yelled 'Shut up!' and hit him hard, to hurt. She'd felt the nipple squashing under his shirt. But he'd looked at her like a scientist in a white coat and said indifferently, 'I don't fight girls.' All pretence, she knew, his playing cool; but somehow he'd won. He knew something.

If he was there now, thought Joanna heavily, pushing the sweet against her teeth, he'd probably be talking brightly to their father and surreptitiously squashing her against the door handle at the same time. She cracked and crunched the sweet and rounded her hands on her chest. Then she stretched her hand slowly across the length of the seat. She flexed her fingers so her nails caught the light, reflecting and containing the white day. Her finger-nails looked competent, neatly finishing off her fingers. Nobody in the back to stop her looking. She thought how some girls painted their nails, garish colours which cracked. Perhaps hers didn't need varnish . . . She slid over into the centre of the seat, and her arms reached from window to window, the space all hers.

As the light softened behind a cloud they passed a well nestling in an ivy-walled corner of a hamlet, with a high rusty architrave like fingers not quite inter-linked.

'All very picturesque, no doubt,' snorted Mr Langley. 'This clinging to the primitive.'

'But you like France, darling?'

'Aspects,' Mr Langley smiled. 'Aspects. Fine anti-quities, good food and wine . . . beautiful young women.' His eyes slid round to his wife, gleaming.

Her laugh was like the chirp of a bird falling out of its nest. She studied the map.

'How much further, Daddy?' said Joanna.

'Look, there's a dolmen!' He pointed up a slight incline. 'We'll have a look'. The car skidded onto the grass.

They felt the sunshine pressing against the chilled air as they got out. Joanna glanced at the pallid ladies' slippers on the verge. Some were crushed beneath the car wheels.

'Now, you remember what a dolmen is?' Her father took her hand as he led them up the track, rich with mud the colour of dried blood. Mrs Langley picked her way awkwardly.

'A burial chamber. Made by the cavemen – well, you know, prehistoric.' Joanna used her free hand to pull her yellow jumper further over her hips. Her stomach ought to be flatter, less like a child's pot belly, she thought; but sometimes it was soothing to cup her hands secretly over it at night.

The track climbed between a field of green wheat and a wood, a fuzz of spotted green saplings and undergrowth. A large bird flapped up, its wings rough-edged. The air was like thin cold glass stretched sheer over some sleeping creature, trying to breathe.

On the gentle brow of the hill one massive rock rode on a circle of smaller stones, dense darkness within. They stood in a line and looked. The wind pulled at Mrs Langley's chiffon scarf and blew Joanna's dark hair across her face. She pushed it back slowly. The stones were pockmarked.

Joanna went nearer and touched the cresting stone. In the hollows were ragged pools of water. As she put her fingers in she felt soft clinging weed and a tiny snail, furled and pointed, drifted by. Joanna pulled out a bit of the green slime, rolling it in her fingers.

'Seaweed,' she said, pleased. Grubbing on the beach all one summer she and Michael had built endless hanging water gardens of weed and shells, and each night the sea licked them all away; but every day they made a finer garden.

'Don't be absurd, Joanna, how could it be seaweed

up here? We're a hundred miles from the sea. It's millions of years since the sea was here.' Mr Langley stepped forward and examined the pools and the rock, and was silent.

The wind trembled in the green wheat. Mr Langley turned from the rocks, his face sightless behind his dark glasses and said nothing.

'How amazing,' breathed Mrs Langley, smiling at Joanna quietly and she leant forward and tucked a stray lock of hair behind her daughter's ear.

'We'd better get going,' Mr Langley said.

By the car stood an elderly woman in deep boots and a chestnut brown coat. She marked the family as they walked down the track, her face large and shadowed, still as an owl as she watched from under the twists of black scarf around her head.

'Bonjour, M'sieur dames,' she nodded.

Mr Langley whipped out the electronic door opener and the switches clicked on the doors. The woman planted herself a few steps from the car, keeping watch on Joanna.

Joanna passed, clutching her fist tight. 'Ah, la petite,' the woman intoned and put a hot hand on her shoulder for a moment. Her voice echoed in Joanna's stomach. Her mother pinched her sleeve to pull her away.

Joanna looked at the woman as she got slowly into the car and the face rested sleepily on her, brown eyes somehow dense with light beneath heavy lids. The woman held her hands out to her, open, like the statues in the churches they visited; and then the woman spoke low and swiftly to her, rounded, deep phrases as full of a meaning she couldn't understand as the sound of waves churning in and out, holding their breath in silence for an instant, just for her, yet heard by everybody.

'Don't dawdle, Joanna. And throw that stuff away now.' Her father sat erect behind the wheel.

Joanna got in and fingered the weed. It was drying now but its tendrils were still clotted with wet earth and held a snail like a baby's finger nail. In the corner of her eye she could see the woman smiling and

59

nodding at her in her brown coat, like her swimming teacher encouraging her to jump in the water.

'We don't want it smelling out the car. It's disgusting.'

Joanna let it drop on the earth, soundlessly, and shut the door.

'Disgusting,' Michael had glared at her. 'Bleeding every month like pee. When you do it you'll have to wear a nappy.' They were in the garden, the lawn suddenly stark and green like a TV advert. Hot, she'd tried to explain how it was about womanhood and babies and how she wanted to start, but he kicked his ball past her and went indoors to talk to their father. The sitting room window flashed back at her.

The woman stood, as the car shrieked off.

'What was she saying, dear?'

'Oh, peasant nonsense about that wretched seaweed and Joanna and good luck. To think that after centuries of one of the finest of European civilizations, people are still riddled with all that old superstition . . .'

'Poor old thing,' murmered Mrs Langley, fingering the map.

'Silly old hag,' said her husband. 'They all get like that, the local women . . . I suppose . . .'

They drove, cutting right and left on roads bare of signs, with only the occasional farm vehicle lumbering along. They wound through a wood of silver birches and larches, amid experimental bird noises and leaves flickering green and yellow, like girls preparing for a party.

Joanna wondered why her father had made her throw away the weed if it brought good luck. Would that spoil it? But there was still a warm patch like sunshine on her shoulder where the woman had touched her, the woman who was saying something to her. Perhaps it was enough just to have found the weed. And, she thought, her father hadn't believed her, but she'd been right. What would the good luck be? Would Michael come home and go to day school . . . ? She looked at her finger nails. She wasn't sure she

60

really wanted him at home now, bullying and showing off . . . It would be nice to have a sister, someone she didn't have to explain things to. She remembered the brown armchair she used to talk to when she was little, warm as when she breathed close on her own skin . . . Anyway, she thought, good luck didn't work if you planned it, you had to let it ripen out of things and surprise you.

A smile was teasing her inside, wanting to burst wider, but she made her mind foggy, trying not to think about anything, and wove her hair across her face so she felt like a witch, peering through the tangles at the glimmers and shadows in the woods.

A clearer light bathed the car as they came out of the woods and stopped outside a crumbling sandstone farmhouse, clutched together with ivy. Irises and golden eyes of wallflowers emblazoned the grass and clusters of lilac brushed over the door like grapes. Mr Langley turned the map around and sighed. Mrs Langley waited and said nothing.

Joanna saw a grey shutter half-open and a slight swell behind a lace curtain patterned with swans. She watched the rich bronze chickens patter in the yard beside the house, where two old cartwheels rested against the barn wall.

Then there was a woman tapping at Mr Langley's window. He opened it slightly wider.

'Je peux vous aider, M'sieur dames?' She was tall, stooping to the car, her face high cheek-boned and wreathed in tender lines, her hair black and streaked with silver, swept back into a fall itself almost like a soft scarf. Joanna saw how her long black clothes shifted in the wind so that somehow the patterns of tiny red flowers almost sparked off on their own, like stars flying.

'Merci, Madame, on ne vous derange pas.' Mr Langley was still, his eyes on the map.

Her hand hovered like a bird on the window. Mr Langley glanced at her again and suddenly swallowed.

'Enfin . . .' he hesitated, 'peut-être vous connaissez Pont du Sec?' His Adam's apple rose and fell as he looked at her and his neck reddened.

She laughed. The sound fell through Joanna's stomach so that she stopped sucking. The woman flung her arm out like some wild dancer and spoke rapidly.

'What's she saying?' Mrs Langley's face was white.

'She does know Pont du Sec ... Obviously this map is wrong,' muttered Mr Langley. He was staring at the woman.

The slight swell behind the lace curtain wavered and thickened.

There was a pause. Mr Langley took off his sunglasses.

The woman was still. She looked at Mrs Langley and Joanna and then consideringly at Mr Langley. 'M'sieur, j'ai quelque chose a vous demander.' Then she spoke quickly, smiling once past Mr Langley at his wife and her eyes lit on Joanna for a moment, dark. In the pit of her stomach Joanna remembered digging for buried treasure at the bottom of the garden with Michael one misty, secret day.

Mr Langley started to get out of the car. 'She wants some help with something,' he nodded at his wife. 'I couldn't make it all out.' As Mrs Langley started to open her door, he added, 'No, it needs a man, she says.' He coughed and was gone, following the woman like a dog into her dim doorway.

'I don't understand.' Mrs Langley watched the space in front of the house.

'I thought he didn't like French people,' said Joanna. 'He's rude to lots of them.'

'Joanna, that's not a nice thing to say about your father,' said Mrs Langley mechanically, still watching. She turned her wedding ring round and round.

Joanna saw the lace curtain slacken. What was her father doing in there? Her insides felt warm and limp. She twisted, running her nails over the rough textured wool of the seat, and watched the house. How could such a tall person live in that curled up little place with its low doorway; and the other person, behind the lace?

The wind had been swallowed up in mid-day silence. It was getting hot. A fly swerved into the car,

62

frantic. They flapped at it until it zoomed out again, and they waited.

'Why don't you go in and see what's happening, Mummy? Shall I?'

'No . . .' said her mother slowly. 'Better not.'

Tall, in black, flecked with red and silver . . . like a witch, the thought flicked through Joanna's mind. There was no other house in sight, only fields; and birdsong, loose in the sky somewhere . . . But it was a long time since she had really believed in witches, though she used to frighten Michael by wrapping herself in a grim old shawl of their grandmother's and making her face go long and crinkly; she'd pull Michael down into the old air raid shelter in the garden, among rotting leaves and the two toads who looked dead but for the breathing in their throats. 'They're princes, I've bewitched them,' she'd gloat, weaving her fingers at Michael, who stood rigid with courage in the doorway of the shelter, his angel's hair lit by the sun outside. 'One day I'll do that to you.' Then Witches and Toads had got mangled into a shrieking game round the lawn, with chasing and falling, devouring and rescuing. Later, Michael invented a version with points and winning. Michael always won, Joanna thought.

But she'd never really believed Michael, or anyone, could be bewitched. Changed. A breath of wind moved the dense purple shadows under the lilac. Her father was odd with that woman; and she thought how his Adam's apple had moved up and down in his throat like the toads breathing.

Her hands felt clammy. And then she saw a flash of blue inside the doorway and then again, a blue dress, a woman with toast brown hair. Two of them then. Inside a woman laughed, like Michael spilling over at a silly Christmas cracker joke. Joanna found it hard to believe they were witches. The chickens were robust and happy, strutting and plucking at the ground as if they knew what they were about, and the flowers looked bright and open. On the washing line two white blouses and some stripy red and white cloths fluttered like cheerful curtains in a doll's house.

63

There was another, airier laugh and Mr Langley hurried out of the doorway. His clothes seemed too big for him, as if he had shrunk. He tumbled into the car.

Mrs Langley was tapping her fingers on the map. Mr Langley looked bewildered. He turned clumsily to his wife.

'She just wanted me to move a wardrobe – massive great Provençal thing – her brother died' – Mr Langley swallowed – 'It was blocking the window at the back – she wanted more light', he gabbled, crashing the gears as he tried to get the car going.

Joanna wondered why he just said 'she' when there were two of them. Perhaps the other one didn't live there.

'Oh,' said Mrs Langley, thoughtfully. 'Are we going to Pont du Sec now?' She pronounced the words as if she had pins in her mouth.

'Pont du Sec? Oh. No. It's behind us anyway. No. No, there's no point. Rosalind . . .' he said slowly, pleading. 'I – I made a mistake. I'm sorry.'

His wife was still for a second. She touched her hair, then laid her hand on his knee and he clasped it and kept it as he drove.

As the car turned a bend Joanna looked back and saw the cottage and barn clustered under dozing red roofs and the two women, the tall one and the one in blue, standing arm in arm on the edge of the road. They looked like two linked hands wearing different coloured gloves. It would be nice to have a sister, she thought again, running her thumb through her hair.

MEMBER OF THE FAMILY

Cherry Potts

It is a Sunday afternoon and the visitors are arriving. Angela is in the hall, rattling keys and gloating over the number of cars churning up the gravel of the drive, which isn't really a car park – all the more to buy her home-baked teas later.

She hasn't opened the door yet, it's only 2.27 by her digital watch, although the grandmother clock (French, eighteenth-century, notice the interesting painting on the face and the upside-down numbers), struck the half-hour two minutes ago. Of course, she (as always) is right.

I pin my 'guide' badge on and struggle up the steep staircase, mind the third step, it's not the same height as the others. I rest at the top, ready to 'do' the upper floor as required by the more inquisitive type. I don't 'do' as heavily as Angela – I can always hear her droning on downstairs, boring their ears off.

I don't know why she always gets to do downstairs, it's me who has trouble with my rheumatics, and she doesn't really know the first thing about it. Well I do know, she *says* its so she can keep an eye on the kitchen and her cakes, but really it's because she doesn't feel comfortable 'doing' the bedrooms.

2.30 – the door opens to an impatient shuffle of card showing, coin rattling, umbrella shaking and stiletto

65

shedding. In under five minutes the ones who can't cope with Angela will be up here, hoping I'm not going to lecture them. I watch them over the bannister rail.

The literary types are peering dutifully at the very dull books in the glass-fronted case in the alcove, and the manuscript (unfinished) in the display case just far enough from the door for security.

The architecture buffs linger over the carvings on the staircase, entwined mermaids; that's why they lived here, because of the mermaids.

The gardeners glance round impatiently and head for the back door, the conservatory and the garden, despite the drizzle.

The I'm-a-members finger the pottery and wall hangings, ignoring the 'do not touch' sign – which cannot possibly apply to them.

The 'raining on holiday'ers are complaining that it's not very big and you'd have thought someone that famous would've lived somewhere, well . . . grand, wouldn't you, and regret having parted with the £2.50 they could have spent at the cinema if they'd known.

Those 'in the know' are blocking the stairs, gazing intently at the photographs: Sarah smiling into the sun, shading her eyes; Clare asleep in a deckchair. Sarah with a dog; Clare gardening in her father's old cap. Sarah and Clare on holiday with an unidentified friend. Of course, I could identify the friend, but I don't think she'd be very pleased. Then there's the one of Sarah and Clare mending the car, or trying to . . . The car that they were driving when . . . well, that car.

Now the first of them have reached me. A tweed-and-shootingstick couple with grandchild (bored) in tow. Rained off life-members at a guess. They look expectantly at me, so I smile. He comments on the cartoon at the top of the stairs. I hate that cartoon, Clare hated it, Sarah hated it, even Angela hates it, but there it sits, because it's 'historically valuable' just to remind you that people hated them, in case you hadn't realised.

I am part way though my witty exposé of the scandal that was responsible for its existence when I see their eyes glaze, although the child is looking more interested, and realise I've said something wrong. I find myself trailing off, saying – of course don't let me keep you from seeing the rest of the house if you aren't interested . . . and imagine Clare making evil eyes at his hurriedly retreating back and throwing imaginary daggers at him. I wonder what it was they objected to.

The next group are hovering, now wanting to be told the official version. Seven or eight women, one of them clutching a sheaf of handwritten notes. They look hopefully at me, willing me out of earshot so that the notebearer can give her lecture in peace. I oblige, but not without an exaggerated favouring of the left leg that is not entirely necessary. I seat myself in the window where I can hear perfectly, there is nothing wrong with my hearing.

They cluster around the doorway to the bedroom and she starts to tell them what little she has managed to glean from the guarded comments that have been published from Sarah's notebooks. Clare never wrote a thing. There are no letters; you don't write to someone you share a bed with every night for thirty odd years.

It's amazing how little they left behind. One best seller of notoriety, three notebooks covering everyday things for about six years; lots of photographs, a small country house with an interesting garden, the odd letter to friends; the unfinished manuscript. That's about all.

I can hear the lecture unfolding along somewhat wishful lines. I walk gently back to them and interrupt. One or two visibly jump.

'I'm sorry dear, but that's not correct at all. An interesting theory of course, but regrettably, nonsense.'

She glares at me with the 'and what would you know about it' expression. So I trot out my credentials: sister of the author, co-benefactor under the will, part-owner of the house. She bristles, and I bet she's thinking I've got loads of letters hidden away, but I haven't. So I explain that it is not true that Sarah had other lovers, that she and Clare were boringly mono-gamous (sorry to disappoint); Rachel was my friend,

and certainly never slept with *Sarah*. One of them
laughs. I warm to the subject, ignoring the faintly
shocked silence that seems to have fallen over the rest
of the house, and even raise my voice a little.

I tell them about the walking holiday Sarah and I
had gone on in 1938, and how Sarah had tripped Clare
up going into a tea shop, in her urgent haste for
something hot and wet.

I tell them how she had then been rude to Clare's
husband Malcolm and then made me apologise for
her. How Clare had copied our address down from the
inside flap of my bird watcher's guide, without saying
anything, and written to us . . .

'Ruby darling, you're causing a terrible blockage on
the stairs,' calls Angela in one of her anxious 'don't be
so obvious' voices, terribly bright and cheerful,
threatening terrible things later.

Of course she is right. I wave them on, suggesting
that Angela's teas are worth a try, and they take the
hint.

Of course, it happens regularly. There are always some
women who really want to know. So I tell them. But I
don't tell them about me. Sarah's the famous one, the
dead one, the one Clare chose. We are entitled to some
secrets in the family still, I hope. Poor Angela would
have a fit if she actually discovered that I had more in
common with Sarah than being her sister. After all
she's only related by marriage.

It's strange how much I miss them still, Sarah and
Clare. Especially Clare. That's partly why I still do this
stupid guide business. Where else is a woman my age,
living in the middle of nowhere, going to meet other
lesbians?

THE VISITORS

Amanda Hayman

'I'm home,' called out Alicen, as she closed the front
door behind her, glad that another busy day was over,
and looking forward to a relaxing evening. If Becky or
Caitlin were home she could hang out with them,
perhaps open a bottle of wine. She hadn't seen much
of them recently.

As she turned to hang up her jacket, the brace that
had supported her left leg since a childhood bout of
polio caught her instep at an uncomfortable angle,
something that had been happening a lot recently. She
ought to go up to the hospital and get it seen to, but
there was never enough time.

'Had a good day?' enquired Becky at Alicen's entry
into the kitchen, looking up from the table where she
was chopping vegetables – a lot of vegetables.
Certainly more than the three of them could eat. Heart
sinking, Alicen remembered the phone call the night
before from 'Lesbian Connection'. A couple were
passing through, they'd said, on their way north, and
wondered if they could drop by. In her usual friendly
manner Becky had invited the two for dinner, and
offered the spare room, should they need it.

Just for a moment Alicen wished that she didn't
share her house with a woman whose mission in life
was to unite the Lesbian nation single-handed. Damn
you Becky, she thought, we hardly ever get a night to

ourselves. But it was too late to complain, and she doubted that Becky would have understood; after all they shared the same goals and ideals, didn't they?

She took a deep breath, and when she replied her voice was as pleasant as she could make it. 'It was OK,' Alicen said, 'long, but not a total loss.'

Becky considered the deep furrow between the older woman's brows, and pulled out a chair. 'Back bothering you again, Allie?' she asked sympathetically. 'Here, sit down, I'll make some tea.'

She left her work and went to the stove, glad of the chance to straighten her tall frame. Jeans were never quite long enough for Becky, and today, as usual, her bony wrists stuck out a couple of inches from the sleeves of her navy sweater.

'Shall I chop?' offered Alicen, determined to make up for her brief flash of irritation. But this Becky would not allow, declaring that twenty minutes of rest was what Alicen needed to revive her.

'Where are these two from?' Alicen wanted to know, inwardly amused that she could recover from her pique enough to be curious in so short a space of time.

Deftly Becky fitted pastry into a pie dish, and trimmed round the edges. 'You know, they didn't say. Funny that, because I'm sure I asked.' She ladled an egg mixture into the case she had prepared, wiping floury hands carelessly on her jeans. 'The woman I spoke to had an accent I couldn't quite place, not from this part of the world.' She smiled at Alicen. 'But she was real pleasant, and so grateful when I said they could stay.'

A sudden thought struck her. 'You don't mind them coming, do you Allie? I just realised I went right ahead and invited them, without a word to you or Caitlin.'

Alicen struggled to be honest, despite the knowledge that Becky would be wounded. 'It's OK this time Becky, but in future, if I'm around when women call like that, I think I would like you to ask.'

'I'm sorry,' Becky said in a low voice, painfully conscious that her exuberance had once more trampled someone else's feelings. And although Alicen had more than an inkling of her distress she kept her own counsel.

It was fortunate, perhaps, that Caitlin chose that moment to arrive at the back door, hot and sweaty, though in good spirits after working in the garden. She stopped on the doorstep and grinned at them. 'Here's another lettuce, and a few tomatoes, but they need ripening up.' Becky took the offerings and put them on the draining board. 'One of the panes in the greenhouse was smashed. Probably a cat, so I've boarded it up with card,' Caitlin continued. 'Someone'll have to fix it properly, but not me. I'm starting a double shift again tomorrow.' She shook her head at Alicen, who was starting to speak. 'Just hold on a tick and I'll be in, as soon as I've got the mud off the tools.' And so saying she disappeared.

Alicen sighed, disturbed by the dark-eyed woman's words. She works too hard, she thought, I must talk to her about it.

As if reading her mind, Becky leant over and gently took her hand. 'Let it go, Allie,' she said, her voice firm. 'Caitlin has to find out for herself that working twenty hours a day won't put the clock back. At any rate, she won't thank you for interfering.'

For a moment they were silent, both remembering how Caitlin had sworn to regain the ten lost years spent in an unforgiving jail for a crime that was no crime at all. Alicen had known her before, since they were both younger than Becky's nineteen years, and it was painful to see how that incarceration had built within Caitlin a fear of any involvement in fighting for their rights. She did it anyway, but never without the watchdog of her past sitting on her shoulder. 'I'll go,' Becky said as the doorbell rang. She wiped her hands on her jeans one more time as she left the room. They heard Becky's voice in the hall, greeting the newcomers and a moment later she ushered them into the kitchen.

'This is Jy, and this is Fliss.' She indicated each woman in turn. 'My housemates, Alicen and Caitlin.'

'Hi.'

'Nice to meet you.'

For an instant the women stared, each trying to place the others in some category or pigeonhole, seeking a basis for communication.

While the others performed the social niceties Caitlin hung back, making an effort not to smile. These two were certainly the epitome of the Lesbian couple salt-and-pepper shaker theory. Why, they were alike enough to be sisters. But on closer examination she realised that they were not, in fact, so very identical. To be sure their hair was the same colour, a most unusual mixture of red and grey. Striped, was the word that came to mind, though it appeared not to be dyed. Both had grey eyes, too, and wore what she secretly thought to be ridiculous black and silver headbands. Their faces were quite different shapes, though, and Jy's hair was long, curling down her back. They were big women, taller than Becky, and under their check workshirts and jeans their full breasts and well-rounded bellies were clearly marked. Despite their barely-lined faces. Caitlin could have sworn that these two had more than her own fifty-one years to their credit. But how could that be?

With a start she realised Alicen was talking to her.

'Want some wine, Caitlin?'

'Oh, yes, yes please.' Heavens, it must have looked rude, her staring and staring like that. She seated herself at the table, and made an effort to join in the conversation, turning to the woman beside her.

'Your name is . . . Jy, is that right?'

'Yes, that's right.'

'That's unusual.'

Jy smiled, as if she'd been told that before. 'It means "conscious",' she said simply, sipping delicately at the glass of wine.

'Where are you from?' Not the most scintillating question, but Caitlin was determined to do her bit. In any case, Jy appeared not to have heard, for she was joining Fliss in answering a question Becky had asked about their travels.

It seemed they'd been on women's land for the last couple of weeks, at Eleven Pines in the mountains three hours' drive to the south, and before that over on the east coast. Caitlin was eager to hear about these places: when she had enough money saved up she was going to get a place for herself, a little farm where women could live peacefully and never see men from one month to the next, if they didn't want to, which she certainly didn't.

Reluctantly she got up to help Becky with the plates, but Fliss waved her back.

'I'll do it,' she insisted, going over to the stove. She was the taller of the two, and with those broad shoulders and hips she put Caitlin in mind of tales of the Amazons, those proud Lesbians who had obeyed no man's word.

'Do the headbands have any special significance?' Direct as ever, Becky spoke out.

Jy touched one hand to her brow. 'They were given to us by a very wise woman.'

'That's right.' Fliss looked back from the potatoes she was serving. 'Long, long ago, and we've never taken them off. She said they would protect us from evil thoughts, and I guess they have.' She turned back to her task.

'Was that in your own country?' asked Alicen.

Jy nodded her agreement.

'Where's that?' Caitlin asked.

'Dinner's up!' Becky and Fliss put an overflowing plate in front of each woman.

'All the vegetables come from our garden,' Alicen told them proudly. 'Caitlin works out there every spare minute she has.'

'Can you grow them organic on city soil?' Fliss was intrigued. 'Isn't it terribly hard?'

Laughing, Caitlin replied. 'Is that what the country dykes told you?'

A trifle embarrassed, Fliss admitted that it was.

'Well, with a lot of love and hard work anything is possible, believe you me,' Caitlin told her.

'We know,' sayd Jy softly. 'I'm so glad that you feel that way too.'

Becky watched and listened as she ate. She felt drawn to these two women. The lift of their voices

73

was so pleasing, and she hadn't worried for a minute that they might patronise her, as was often the case when everyone was so much older. She was glad they were staying the night, it would give her more time to talk to them.

'But I'm not sure I believe that all separatists should go and bury themselves in the country.'

A comment from Jy brought Becky into the conversation.

'Oh, neither do I,' she said eagerly. 'How can we pass on all that we've learnt if we're so far away from the dykes who are considering separatism as an option?'

'Go to it, Becky,' said Alicen. 'There are a lot more Lesbians round here willing to listen to me since you came along. Left to ourselves, Caitlin and I are entirely too hermit-like.'

Caitlin snorted. 'Keen on protecting ourselves from trashing and sensation-seekers, more like. I ask you, does a Lesbian hang round straight women in the hope that they'll learn from her?' This was an on-going dispute between her and Becky, one they enjoyed very much indeed, each with her hopes of converting the other to her way of thinking.

A hum of laughter went round the room. 'And what about you. Alicen?' asked Jy. 'What do you think about the "love them or leave them" dichotomy?'

'For me to decide to live in the country would depend,' Alicen began slowly, 'on how much the quality of my life would be improved. If I believed I would be healthier, and not so troubled by this,' she motioned towards her left leg, 'then, yes, I think I would move. But only if it was a sizable community. You see I have a great affection for all the Lesbians who I know in this town, even if I don't spend a lot of time among them. I probably have more contact with dykes passing through, but it makes me feel good when I hear about how Robby and friends have been harassing the pigs or the porn merchants, and I can say to myself, I know her. She's a good woman, even if we don't always see eye to eye. And we're working for the same thing in the end.' She stopped to take a breath. 'If you see what I mean.'

'I do.' Jy put her hand over Alicen's. 'It sums up perfectly how I feel about the dykes in my community.'

'Where's that?' asked Caitlin.

'In fact,' Jy went on, rising from the table, 'there's something from home in my bag that you might like to see.' She went towards the door.

'Why don't I show you your room?' suggested Becky shyly.

'Oh, but what about the dishes?' Fliss was ready to help again, but Caitlin stepped in to return the earlier favour.

'My turn,' she said. 'You go with Becky.' I need to think, and washing up is one of the best aids to clearheadedness I know. Something strange is going on here.

Aloud she said, 'It's OK Allie. I'll clear the table. You go and listen to the oohs and aahs about that guest room you've taken so much trouble with.'

Stopping only to caress Caitlin's cheek, Alicen went.

Over the dirty pans, Caitlin pondered. What *is* it, she asked herself, this thing that I can't put my finger on? Something isn't right. The young faces when they obviously aren't, those ridiculous headbands, the way they somehow managed to avoid saying where they came from. And yet, it isn't a *bad* strangeness. She'd bet her life on that. Ten years behind prison walls with only her wits between her and a vast range of horrors had given Caitlin a keen sense of who was to be trusted. These two were OK, she was sure. Somehow they'd managed to connect with her, and Becky, and even Alicen, who'd opened up in a truly remarkable way.

Even now, Caitlin realised, fishing in the soapy water for forgotten spoons, I'm looking forward to them coming back into the room. They don't sparkle, or demand attention. It's more of a warm, steady glow that you notice after a while. Centred. That's it. They're centred in a way that I'd like to be.

Down the stairs floated the sound of footsteps, and

voices growing louder. No doubt Fliss and Jy had found that the accommodation here was a good deal more luxurious than that of the last couple of weeks. And why not? Each to her own taste was a maxim Caitlin was fond of quoting, and if Alicen chose to spend her money on curtains and carpets, well, that was up to her.

'And there was a tiny waterfall that fed the swimming hole. It was the pleasantest place you could hope to find.' Fliss was telling some tale of a land tract they had been to. 'But the most extraordinary thing was that those women commute everyday, an hour or more by car into the city, to the same jobs they always had.'

'They think they've got the best of both worlds.' added Jy.

'But you don't think so, right?' commented Alicen shrewdly.

Jy laughed heartily, the first time they'd heard her do so. The red and grey curls danced and bounced around her face, and she swept them away with a careless hand. 'Well, maybe they have, and maybe they haven't. In any case, it isn't nice to criticise folks when they so kindly offer you hospitality, now is it?'

'And how about the folks back home?' Not expecting to be answered, Caitlin went on 'Herb tea or coffee for you Jy?'

Grey eyes flew open wide, to meet the gaze of her black ones. But Caitlin did not look away. 'Tea or coffee?' she repeated.

'Tea, please.'

'For me, too,' said Fliss quietly.

'You've asked about our home several times Caitlin.' Jy was quite serious now.

Caitlin put mugs around the table, seating herself opposite the two. 'That's right,' she agreed. 'But you haven't answered me yet.'

Becky was mystified. 'Why on earth not?' she wanted to know. 'It's not a secret, is it?'

'"Why on earth" is not a very good phrase to use, as it so happens,' Fliss told her. 'Because, you see, this is not where we're from.'

76

She sat back, glad of Jy's presence beside her. What would the reaction be this time?

'Sorry?' Alicen was frankly nonplussed. 'So where *are* you from?'

'From Cerridwen Seven, which is the third planet of the star Meiripides, in the system of Sapphia,' Jy answered softly.

A great snort of laughter greeted this statement.

'Oh come on,' guffawed Caitlin. 'You don't really expect us to swallow that?'

Jy said nothing. This was always the difficult part.

'The system of Sapphia,' repeated Caitlin. 'I'm sorry to be rude, Jy, but it's got to be a joke.'

Still the two were silent.

Becky looked from one to the other. 'How old are you?' she asked.

'Older than you can imagine,' said Fliss. 'Thousands of your earth years, if you want a number.'

'But .... how?'

'We never die,' explained Fliss gently, 'unless we meet an accident, or choose to stop our lives and start over again. There's always that option.'

'Bit crowded on that planet, isn't it?' Caitlin's cynicism was crushing.

'But we have a whole star system to expand into. More space than we could fill in a billion, billion light years.'

Slowly a memory stirred in Alicen. Tales she had heard from time to time from dykes, well, fairy stories really, about how Lesbians came from a different place, were not natives of this war-torn, misogynist planet.

'A Lesbian planet?' she asked in a whisper.

'Far more than a planet. And yes, Lesbian of course. For there are no males in Sapphia.'

'Did we come from there?' It was a hard question for Alicen to ask, but harder still not to.

Jy shook her head. 'No you did not. Lesbians on earth are a wonderful, miraculous occurrence, the like of which we have not found elsewhere in all of time and space.'

The five women sat around the table, tea cooling

before them. Fliss and Jy knew better than to volunteer information – they were not here as missionaries. As for Alicen, Caitlin and Becky, it was a situation for which they were woefully unprepared.

Caitlin was struggling hard. She'd known they were strange, yes. But *aliens*? Good women, a tiny voice reminded her. Why should they want to trick you? She cleared her throat. 'Um . . . you took me by surprise. I'm sorry. Do you think you could tell us *why* you're here, if you're who you say you are. That might make it a bit easier to understand.'

'This is not the first time we've visited earth,' Fliss began. 'If you are to understand you need to know a little of the history that binds our worlds together. May we try to tell you?'

The three gave their assent.

'As Jy said, it was most unexpected that Lesbians be among the inhabitants of planet earth. We knew it as a place for the unholy, warmongering humans, and left you strictly to yourselves. Until . . .'

'Until,' Jy took up the story, 'there came a time when a group of women made themselves too autonomous and too powerful for their masters' liking. They were proud and strong, and they fought battles against the men for the right to live their lives as they pleased, taking land and defending it with ease. Worst of all, they had no need of men in any way, finding love and ecstasy in each other's arms.'

'The Amazons,' breathed Becky.

'Yes, the Amazons.' It was Fliss's turn again now. She and Jy seemed to know without signals who would speak next.

'If their existence is acknowledged at all, it is as a race who were totally destroyed by the men they angered. But it was not so. Many hundreds came with us to Sapphia, leaving behind for good the carnage they knew on earth.'

She paused, searching the faces of the women in front of her. They would believe eventually, she was certain. She and Jy would not have come otherwise. But time was of the essence, and she could not wait for them to come round at their own pace.

'Go on,' urged Caitlin.

Jy continued. 'The next time we came was in your fifteenth century. Once more Lesbians demanded that they be allowed to lift the yoke of servitude to men. This time it was skills of healing and spiritual awareness that brought disaster upon their heads. Again, Lesbians were victims of a systematic destruction that sought to denounce them as perpetrators of the very evil they were intent upon eradicating. History says that nine million women across the continent of Europe died horribly at that time, taking with them the secrets of the witches.'

'Are you saying they weren't murdered?' Becky couldn't believe her ears.

'I wish that were true.' Jy looked sad. 'In fact, millions did die. And make no mistake, their biggest crime was loving women, the crime that across the ages men have always found truly unforgivable. The numbers that you have learnt, however, include those that inexplicably disappeared, but in the terrible confusion of the age such details were not documented. Their knowledge lives still in Sapphia.'

'And now you're here again.' Alicen's voice was flat, lifeless, causing Becky and Caitlin to turn to her in alarm. 'Does that mean that our lives as Lesbians are threatened?' She felt as if it was another speaking, so unemotional was the tone. Hadn't she talked with a friend, more than once, of how one day the burning times would return, with Lesbians as the target?

Fliss got up and went to Alicen's side, kneeling to put an arm around her. 'Yes Alicen, we believe danger is approaching. Maybe not this year, perhaps not for five. But you must know as well as we that all the signs are there.' She stroked Alicen's hair. 'Will you come home with us?'

'What, me?'

'Yes, you, and Caitlin and Becky.'

'To Sapphia?'

'Yes.'

'You're serious aren't you?' Caitlin spoke.

'We are, Caitlin,' said Jy, reaching out a hand to her and one to Becky.

79

Caitlin took the hand and examined it carefully. It seemed identical to her own, except for the size. The café au lait skin was soft, with none of the signs of age Caitlin's hand had collected. 'Are you human?' she asked.

Jy shook her head. 'No, we're Lesbians.'

'What do you mean?'

'That's the name of our people. You took it from us, you see'.

Oh goddess, thought Caitlin, let me wake up, this is stranger than I ever suspected. She hunched into her chair pulling away her hand.

'Caitlin?' She doesn't like it, thought Fliss. We need to allay her suspicions. 'What do you need to know?' The ones who had suffered most were always the last to accept that Sapphia existed.

'I need proof,' burst out Caitlin. 'I'm sorry,' – this as Alicen and Becky protested – 'but I do. What if I decide I'll believe in you, that I want to go to this wonderful Lesbian existence, set my mind to leave everything I know, and then when I wake up in the morning you're gone, a couple of charlatans who were having a laugh?'

Getting to her feet, Jy went to the dresser, on which she had placed a small box of smooth, polished wood when she returned downstairs. She placed it in the middle of the table. 'I said I had something from home to show you,' she said.

Fliss leant over and opened the latch that secured the top, then reached inside. Out came something wrapped in a soft, creamy cloth that seemed, unaccountably, to be breathing. Inside, safely nestling, was a globe of glass a litte bigger than a tennis ball. Carefully, she spread the cloth on the table, then set the treasure down.

'What is it?' Caitlin wanted to know.

Fliss looked from face to face. Caitlin, frowning, glancing sideways at the ball. Alicen, pale, her small face vulnerable and a little afraid. And Becky, eyes shining, staring with wonder.

'Becky knows,' she said. 'Don't you Becky?'

Becky did. She'd seen a sphere like this once when

she was very small, in the room of her great grandmother, the one who spoke no English.

'It's a crystal ball,' she murmured.

'For fortune telling?' In her surprise Alicen forgot to be frightened.

Once more Jy's lovely laugh reverberated around the room. 'It depends what you mean by fortune, Alicen.' She tapped the glass lightly with her index finger. 'Won't you take a look?'

As Alicen watched the sphere became opaque, clouded with a fast-moving swirl of dusky colours whirling together. By and by it began to clear.

'Look, Alicen.'

Awkwardly Alicen manoeuvred herself into a position directly above the crystal ball. At first she could make out only smudges, hints of figures, maybe, or trees but as she focused a scene formed before her eyes.

In the foreground were two people, women, sitting on a rock, their legs hanging down towards a pool of dark water. They were holding hands, and talking in low voices. One had skin of a tawny brown, her straight, red-grey hair forming a cloak to below her waist. The other was lighter by far, her naked body the bright white of ice, but her hair was of the same curious mixed shade. A line of the same coloured hair ran from her pubis up her belly as far as the valley between her breasts, more like fur really, and as she moved the short hairs glistened in the moonlight.

Moonlight! All at once Alicen became aware of the vista surrounding the pair. Not one, but three moons lit the scene. In the upper right portion of the brilliant turquoise sky was a large, dark circle, completely dwarfing the light-giving moons in size.

As she stared, the women stopped talking, and the pale one turned her head.

'Hello, Alicen,' she said pleasantly, and for the first time Alicen saw that an area above the bridge of her nose was glowing, pulsing gently all the while.

She could not speak, but the woman went on. 'My name is Epp, and this is the world from which Jy and Fliss have come.' She stood up and indicated the

81

landscape. Now Alicen could see that other women were there, bustling to and fro, hear a phrase or two of female voices singing.

'You are welcome here, among the Lesbians,' Epp assured her. 'Life is sweet when you are free to find out who you really are.'

'Please take care,' the dark woman spoke for the first time, her voice clear and melodious, 'when choosing your fortune, dear Alicen. Be sure that there is no doubt in your heart about leaving the old ways behind, for that is essential to your fulfilment here.'

She held out her hands, and the spot on her forehead pulsed faster. 'I am Yua. Remember me,' her voice said in Alicen's head. But she had not spoken. Had she?

Dazed, Alicen stumbled backwards, glad of Fliss's strong arm guiding her into a chair. A glass of water was put into her hand and she sipped it gratefully, dimly aware that Becky was now looking into the crystal globe. Would that woman . . . Epp? . . . know her name too?

Caitlin was last, and more prepared. She spoke to Yua and Epp for several minutes, asking them questions, then continued to look in silence, though a myriad of expressions flitted across her face. At last, exhausted, she flopped onto the couch at the side of the room, her features grim.

Becky, however, was already recovering from her surprise, and gripping Jy's arm, declared, 'I'll go. It's what I've always wanted, I know that. Oh wow, it's so thrilling, I can't wait.'

'Becky, you mustn't decide so quickly.' Such elation was not unusual, but if taken at face value could be disastrous, and Jy was anxious to avoid any mistakes. 'If you decide it's what you want, that's wonderful, but please, please think deeply about what you would be leaving first. You see, there can be no return. Ever.'

Fliss looked at Alicen. She would be alright, her colour was already starting to come back. The two women of the planet Cerridwen Seven stood up.

'We will go to bed shortly,' Jy said. 'In the morning

we hope that you will give us your answers. Whatever you choose should be the best thing for *you*. There is no right or wrong. We beg that you decide for yourself, by yourself, so that you are quite, quite sure in your own mind.'

'But wait!' Alicen didn't have enough information to make such a momentous decision.

They turned sapphire eyes towards her questioningly.

'When would we go, and *how*? Are any of the Lesbians in your solar system disabled, like me? Can we choose where, or with whom we will live?'

Jy sat down again, so her face was on a level with Alicen's. 'There is so much you want to know, and yet none of it is necessary. You have to want to go enough that none of that is important. We are Lesbians. We will welcome and cherish you as the rare and wonderful anomaly in the universe that you are. We have no concept of war, no rape, no abuse of our children. We encompass a thousand variations of body and soul without discrimination. Life can be anything you want it to be, but you cannot return. Ever.'

She drew the crystal ball towards her, and lovingly repacked it in the box.

'Take off your headband.' Caitlin's voice was harsh. 'I have to see for myself.'

Slowly Fliss put her hands behind her head and untied the strip of black and silver. And there, between her brows, was the pulsing oval. Caitlin made a move, as if to touch it, but Fliss caught her by the wrist.

'No. You must not do that. It would hurt me, as it would you if I put my finger in your eye.'

'My eye?'

'Yes. This is an eye onto the psychic world. You too have the capabilities it brings, but in an atmosphere of such hatred it would be suicide to develop them.'

'You felt it, Caitlin,' Jy reminded her. 'Didn't you communicate with Yua without words?'

She had. It was true. All this was true, and it made Catlin very angry, though she could not say why.

'Now we must sleep.' Jy tucked the wooden box under her arm. 'Will you meet us here at six in the morning, to tell us your chosen paths?'

Becky, Caitlin and Alicen were appalled. Only seven hours to make the most far-reaching decision of their lives. Still, they nodded in agreement. What else could they do?

Caitlin took herself out onto the back porch with a pack of cigarettes. She hadn't smoked since she got out, but tonight she needed the reassurance of the butt between her fingers. She sat in the old blue armchair, put her feet up on the railing, and stared at the sky. It was a clear night, and hundreds of stars were visible. Somewhere up there . . .

'No, fuck it, it isn't possible.' She flung the expletive across the darkened garden. Now she knew why she was angry. She needed that safety, the freedom from worry of what men would do next, so very, very much. She would never forgive them for the ten years they had stolen.

A man rapes a women in her own home, threatens her at gunpoint so she'll comply then runs off into the night. The next day she seeks him out and shoots him. Not dead, you understand, but in such a way to make sure he won't be able to repeat his actions. *He* was never brought to trial for his crime, but she was locked away, because she had dared to fight back. On god, what wouldn't she give for a place like Sapphia?

Everything, that's what. Because she wanted it *here*, on earth, in the way she'd always planned it. The farm she dreamed about so many hours of the day. And now she would never have it, because if what those two said was true, then she'd spend the rest of her days on this planet fighting. Fighting to live as a Lesbian, or suffering the consequences of who-knew-what god-awful punishment they dreamed up for women like her this time. The Amazons were forced to marry their captors, the witches burned alive. Women-loving would never be forgiven, and more than anything else, those words inclined Caitlin to believe Jy and Fliss. Ten years, if she'd only had those ten years, she would have lived at least a little of her dream.

She lit another cigarette. Supposing she said 'yes' and they took her away, if they really could do it. Another huge change – one day you're living your life, and suddenly bang, the door slams, it's finished, and you have to start again somewhere else. Caitlin shivered, looked around. Her eyes fell on the garden, so carefully tended day after day. Would she be able to grow things wherever she ended up? And share the space with someone else? She could never do that. It was possible, of course, that in a safe place she wouldn't need so badly to be on her own. Women untainted by the stain of misogyny, what might they be like?

Jy's words ran through her head. 'We are Lesbians, we will welcome and cherish you ... There is so much you need to know and none of it necessary.'

Oh, it was all so hard. Stay and fight, or step off the cliff into the void? How could she ever make a choice?

Excitement heady as mead coursed through Becky's veins as she pranced into her little room. A Lesbian planet! No, more than that, a whole Lesbian universe, more or less. Oh joy, oh heaven, thank you goddess for giving me this chance. Of course she would go, why wouldn't they let her say so there and then?

They were so wonderful. Tall Fliss, with her dimples and gentle smile, the caretaker of the pair, and Jy, more talkative, determined everything should be clear. Imagine if she had a woman like that for a lover, to work with, to plan and plot the overthrow ...

Oh. Becky stopped and sat down on the bed. There would be nothing and no one to overthrow. No men, no patriarchy. What an extraordinary idea. And, presumably, if everyone was a dyke there was no need for networking either. So much of Becky's life was taken up with these activities that she couldn't imagine being without them.

What would I do with all that time? she wondered. Presumably they worked. They must do for the planet to survive. But so many things would be beyond her comprehension. Never mind, she'd learn. She rubbed the space between her heavy black brows, remembering how Fliss had showed them her third eye. She wanted to make hers work, too. That would be something.

Who would she be without the meetings, the letters and newsletters, conferences to plan and festivals to attend? Would those magical psychic skills she was going to learn fill the void that would undoubtedly be left in her heart? Had she used Lesbianism as a way of avoiding the confrontation with herself, to find out what was, or was not, inside?

'What do I want?' she asked her reflection in the mirror, looking at last deep into her own eyes. She delved deeper, but the answer was not there to be divined. But neither was anything unpleasant, much to her relief. Perhaps she would be able to live with herself in that far away place, even believe that she was as nice as her mother said.

Of course there was that to think about. Becky loved her mother and sisters; this would mean never seeing them again, or Liz, or Penny. Not visiting very often was quite different from not having the opportunity at all. She always knew they were there, that she could call if she needed someone to talk to, borrow some money or wail about her job.

She wondered how they'd been chosen. Or maybe they hadn't, it was just chance and being in 'Lesbian Connection' that brought Jy and Fliss here. They'd never said how much she could take with her; probably not everything she'd want, so she'd better starts sorting. But first she'd go and ring her mother. It was the middle of the night, but they wouldn't mind. Softly she opened the door, and was halfway down the stairs before she remembered Jy's words about choosing by themselves.

At first Alicen was sure there was nothing for her to think about. She wouldn't be going, and that was that. She tidied the kitchen and made herself another pot of tea, then went into the living room. It was her favourite place in a house she loved, the room on which she'd lavished most time and attention. The bay window looked out onto the tree-lined street, and the padded window seat was exactly the right height for gazing out, a pastime that pleased Alicen greatly. The furniture had been carefully chosen, a piece at a time; when she found something that was exactly right she went ahead and bought it. On the walls, were photographs of friends, past and present, framed and hung to catch the best light. Many of those women had helped to make this haven what it was, and a good few had lived there.

Life in this town was good to Alicen, better than she had ever dreamed she would achieve, and while she believed Epp's words that life was sweet on her planet, she would never leave here.

She sat down in her spot, the right corner of the sofa, tea on the table beside her. As the brace once more bit into her leg, Alicen cried out involuntarily, biting her lip. She was tired, had been up too long, that was all, she lied to herself, knowing all the while that her support was no longer adequate.

As an eight-year old she had fought against the words condemning her to a wheelchair for the rest of her life, and had proved all the doctors to be wrong. Well, they hadn't known that to Alicen the spectre of being at the mercy of other people was a fate worse than death. They had warned her, though, that as she grew older the sheer willpower which kept her walking might not be enough. That was the real reason she was postponing her visit to the hospital. One day in the not-too-distant future she would have to accept the confinement that to her spelled defeat, over-whelmed at last by the invalidism she had fought for so many years.

She could not take the risk of being in an unknown place where she, or others, found her disability too much to cope with. So often when she was younger she had envied her friends as they decided whether or not to take part in some outing or activity. For her there had not been a choice: it was so often made for her by a world that could not accommodate difference. All her life it had been that way. So many things she might've done, it simply wasn't fair. Why her? Why, why, why? Alicen put her head on the arm of the sofa and cried for all those lost opportunities.

For how long she cried she didn't know, but when she finally stopped she felt a bit better. It was many years since she'd cried over the losses of her youth, not since Paula went away. It was over ten years since their differences had finally become irreconcilable, but she could remember so well what her sweet-faced lover had said.

You have a choice, Paula had told her. You always have a choice, even if it isn't the same as other people's, nor so easy. But if you give up that choice, write yourself into the role of victim, manipulated by a big cruel world, then you give away your power.

Paula was right. To choose was empowering. Alicen remembered the warmth she had felt when Epp spoke to her. She believed in the existence of the faraway planet, she really did. Could she put away the fears that had dogged her younger days and take the risk of travelling to an unknown place? Supposing that circumstances there would lessen the burden of her disability? She tried to imagine what the thousand differences that Jy had mentioned could be. And just how had those women managed to do away with discrimination? Alicen found it impossible to conceive of a place where she was treated exactly the same as everybody else. Imagine not planning an evening around places to sit down, or constantly fending off the pitying looks her limp always drew. Somewhere she would never need help in the course of her daily life, or be required to reassure the able-bodied through their embarrassment with her disability. Somewhere she wouldn't be special.

Shocked, she examined that last idea, knowing deep down that it was not entirely new. Once or twice before she had suspected herself of using her disability to her own advantage, but had never allowed the thought access to her conscious mind. Maybe just sometimes it had been a relief not to have to actively choose her course of action, but to assume the answer to be a given. Those lost opportunities she'd been crying over – she could think of at least one example, where if she was totally honest she would have to say she hadn't really wanted to be included.

Memories surfaced of a proposed trip, when she was seventeen. The members of the school choir had had the opportunity to go to Europe, but Alicen had refused immediately. Too hard a trip for someone like her, she'd said, and smiled bravely. Her friends had felt bad for her, and brought back presents and postcards by way of compensation. She knew, though, that the idea of being with that chattering, giggling group for twelve days non-stop had appalled her. There would never have been anywhere to hide when the heart-stopping shyness overcame her, and she had to be alone. Imagine if she'd had to tell her friends that she didn't *want* to go! Her weak leg had guaranteed that her decision wouldn't be questioned, and wasn't that special treatment?

She sipped the cold tea on the table beside her, and considered a different angle. What was it like to be ordinary? But I'm not ordinary – no one really is, a voice inside her head insisted. Think of all the things I've achieved. I'd stand out even if I walked without trouble. It was true. Once she might have needed to use her weak leg because she lacked the confidence to make sure her needs were met, but not any more. It was like finding a treasure chest within herself, this acknowledgment of her own worth. An overhaul of her self-image was long overdue, and needed taking care of before she could assess tonight's offer with any clarity. Purposefully, Alicen went across to the desk in the corner and began to write.

At this time of year dawn came early. By five o'clock the eastern sky was lightening, and the birds beginning to sing. How still the world was, so early in the day. Becky believed that it had been like this always, before humans evolved.

It had been harder to make a decision once she realised that she could not speak to her mother. To leave without saying goodbye might be what it would amount to, and Becky would not have been human if

89

she had not minded that. Wouldn't have been Lesbian. She played with the words, turning the implications over and over in her mind. If she really did go to Sapphia would she still be human? Or could you become a naturalised member of another species? Naturalisation is a patriarchal idea, she berated herself. You'll have to lose a lot of those.

She had spent the last few hours turning the contents of her room upside down. When you are changing your life so radically, nothing material has much meaning anymore. When it came down to it, there was nothing important enough to take. No photos, because she wanted to look forward, take advantage of every possibility that came her way. Past writing, maybe, but it wouldn't help with the acquiring of a new mindset. One thing had become very clear, however. Whether she went or stayed her life would never be the same again, and that in itself was disturbing.

Caitlin was watching the dawn come up from the strawberry patch, as she smoked the last of her cigarettes. Whoever of them *did* go with Jy and Fliss would not be seeing that tender sight many times more. They would leave soon, she was sure, or why the necessity to decide at a moment's notice? What would happen to the house if they *all* left? She had no friends besides these two, but no doubt Becky would have a contact she could call on.

She laughed at those thoughts. In a bizarre sort of way it was like making arrangements for your own funeral, which few people ever did. She coughed richly, feeling her lungs dragging within her chest. Go or stay, no more smokes, she told herself firmly. That's one form of death I can do without.

The clock on the wall moved relentlessly towards the hour of six, and Alicen urged herself to write faster. Beside her on the desk was a pile of paper, covered on both sides with her small, even handwriting. There was so much she wanted to say, it was as if a restless flood had finally been released. She had not yet confronted the decision that was now only minutes away, for there had been too many self-realisations clamouring for attention.

.And yet, as she wrote, Alicen was aware that some portion of her mind was working out what her reply to the Sapphians' offer should be. She was confident that it would be the right one for her. Her pen flew faster across the page, setting out the details gleaned from forgotten memories. Always, always, she would be thankful to Fliss and Jy, if only for tonight.

At exactly six o'clock the two women from Sapphia descended the stairs, murmuring in low tones, their small, neat packs on their backs. As they entered the kitchen Fliss took Jy's hand. Her anxiety was for each woman to choose wisely, for time had shown that only those who truly had no regrets would flourish.

Alicen, Becky and Caitlin sat round the table drinking tea, as they had done so many times before. Two empty mugs sat next to the teapot, which Becky filled.

Jy and Fliss did not sit down.

'It is time,' Jy said seriously, though her eyes were warm. 'We are ready to learn how each of you has decided.'

THE PRICKLY WITCH

Helen Smith

The prickly witch was busy with her work. She was so hard at work planting a woodland drift of bluebells and ramsons that she didn't notice the greedy girl watching her. Inadvertently she allowed the girl glimpses of her face.

She only looked up from her work when the greedy girl was very close to her, smiling shyly and holding a hand out to the witch. The prickly witch stepped quickly back, and quickly back again. Handfuls of small white bulbs fell at her feet as she raised her open hands against the girl. The greedy girl's smile faltered, but her reaching hand, palm upwards, was steady.

The witch fled. After a time she paused, thinking to have left the girl far behind, but the greedy girl nearly caught her and the witch had to sprint to get away. Listening carefully she could hear the girl's feet running along behind her, and as the witch felt herself begin to tire the girl's footsteps were always there.

The witch's tiredness grew. Her legs felt heavy and her chest ached. She turned her thoughts from her pain to find an answer, to find some way of stopping her pursuer. An idea came to her and suddenly, as she ran, green living canes sprang up in her footsteps, and ripe red raspberries sprang from the canes. The witch paused on the far side of the tangle of raspberry canes and peered through the leaves to see what the greedy girl would do. The greedy girl paused and looked with pleasure at the raspberries. She picked one and popped it into her mouth and smiled. She picked herself a handful of the raspberries. The prickly witch smiled and tiptoed away from the raspberry canes and returned to her work.

She had finished the planting of a bank leading down to a small stream when she was disturbed again. Muttering, and footsteps, running and pausing, then running and pausing again. The witch could hear the greedy girl saying, 'The raspberries were a trick, she tricked me with the raspberries. I mustn't be tricked by raspberries again.'

The witch was amused and stood and watched the greedy girl, and somehow she forgot to conceal herself, until, once more, the girl caught sight of her. Again the girl smiled. If possible the smile was wider than it had been for the raspberries; and she moved towards the witch.

The prickly witch turned and ran away. The greedy girl's footfalls were close behind her and soon the witch began to tire. She didn't want to be caught. 'This time,' she thought, and as she thought green bushes sprang up in her tracks. Amongst the green leaves of the green bushes grew round, black berries. The witch paused on the far side of the carpet of green bushes to see what the greedy girl would do. The greedy girl paused and looked closely at the bushes. She ran one hand through the leaves nearest to her and she smiled her pleased smile. Her hand went to her mouth and then she crouched down and started picking the plump black bilberries. The prickly witch smiled and tiptoed away from the bilberry patch and returned to her work.

A little later she was disturbed once more. There was the muttering again, and the footsteps, running and pausing.

'The bilberries were a trick, she tricked me with the bilberries,' the muttering voice was saying. 'I mustn't be tricked by fruit bushes again.'

The prickly witch jumped up and as she did so the girl caught sight of her. The witch did not wait to see if the girl would smile but started to run straight away.

She could hear the greedy girl's footsteps running along behind her and after a while, as she began to tire, she wondered what would happen if she allowed herself to be caught. She dismissed that thought and turned her mind to evading her pursuer. A tangle of green hoops and arches sprang up behind her, and on every bramble sprouted black and purple blackberries.

The witch heard a shout. 'I'm not stopping for the blackberries,' called the girl. The witch turned around. The greedy girl was struggling through the blackberry bushes, their whippy branches were catching at her clothes and there were long red scratches on her arms and face. But she did not pause to eat any of the beautiful blackberries.

The witch thought about the girl's surprising determination for a moment and she looked once more at the marks on the girl's face. All too soon the greedy girl emerged from the thickest part of the blackberry patch and the witch could see that she was smiling her smile.

'Time to be off,' the prickly witch told herself severely, and took to her legs.

Soon she could hear the girl running along behind her and the witch felt as if she were drawing on her last reserves of strength. As she thought of an excuse that could throw off pursuit, a stand of young trees sprang up in her footsteps. The trees grew quickly and thickly until they towered behind the witch. As she paused to see what would happen, a wind blew through the tops of the trees and the wood filled with the sound of falling nuts. The floor of the wood was covered with shiny black and rotten husks and from the husks peeped the green shells of young walnuts.

The prickly witch watched the greedy girl. The girl did not stop to investigate the walnuts or to crack their soft shells in her fingers, but she was not smiling either and she ran aimlessly from one tree to another, and even ran in circles.

'She doesn't know what walnuts are,' thought the witch, 'or she would stop and eat them, surely.' Being tired, and seeing that the girl had sat down under a tree, the witch made herself comfortable in a clump of bracken at the edge of the wood and went to sleep.

The witch did not know this but the greedy girl knew all about walnuts and their young pale shells and their sweet contents. She knew almost all there was to know about food, which is how she had come by her name. She had been distracted from her pursuit of food, by her pursuit of the witch, for some time but now she felt that this distraction had led her into a dangerous place. She was frightened that she might get lost but she decided to calm herself and to sit down for a while and to think.

She thought carefully about returning to her home, and she thought carefully about the prickly witch. Below her, peeping through the trees she could see the valley where her home lay. She stood up then. If she walked downhill she would come to the valley, and if she walked uphill she might be following the path that the witch had taken. She turned her steps uphill.

In time she passed the bed of bracken where the witch lay sleeping and she saw the witch straight away. The girl made no move, but stood watching the witch, and could have done so for a long time, drinking in the true form of the prickly witch through her greedy eyes.

The witch awoke to find the girl's eyes upon her. She lay still and returned the look. Then she spoke.

'Why have you been following me?' She sounded truly perplexed.

'I saw you,' said the girl simply, and she smiled her smile of pleasure and added, 'You give me wonderful presents.'

She pulled her hand out from her bag and on her palm lay raspberries and bilberries. She held them out to the prickly witch, who took them and put them in her mouth. They were juicy and sweet and their flavours tingled on her tongue.

The greedy girl reached her hand into her bag again and produced, held between finger and thumb, a pale shelled walnut.

She was laughing. 'I could hardly resist this gift,' she said, and handed it to the witch.

'But the scratches on your face,' said the prickly witch.

'Scratches?' said the girl.

'The scratches the brambles gave you,' said the witch.

'I never felt them,' said the girl, and as she spoke the long red scratches healed and were gone.

The witch turned the walnut in her fingers and slowly cracked it. As she raised her eyes, she saw the girl had moved very close to her indeed.

Instead of putting the white walnut into her mouth,

the prickly witch leaned forward and kissed the greedy girl.

The girl did not smile, as the witch had intended her to, but said, 'Yes. More kisses.'

The prickly witch leapt to her feet and, as swiftly as ever before, began to run. The greedy girl sat open-mouthed and watched her. The prickly witch was speeding across rough grassland up ahead, dodging the grey and white stones which lay across her path.

Tears began to slide down the greedy girl's face. For a time it was as if her eyes were melting, but the greedy girl could not cry for ever and besides, there might be a glimpse of the prickly witch still to be seen. She wiped her face on her shirt sleeve and saw that where the witch had run, among the grey and white boulders, across the rough grass, was now a trail of nodding blue and white flowers. They were springing up, spires of blue bells and balls of white flakes, in the footsteps of the prickly witch.

The greedy girl sniffed and walked towards the flowers. Bluebells and wild garlic were good companions, but they were out of season now, and out of place in this rough and open grassland. She bent to catch the smell from a bluebell. It was a green and lively smell which made her think of nakedness and spring rain. She picked a leaf of the wild garlic and rubbed it under her nose. Its warm scent reminded her of meals eaten by firelight at a strong wooden table. She put some leaves in her bag for later.

She wondered if the witch intended her to read a meaning in the flowers, in their colour or in their scent and, if so, what the meaning was. She looked again at the open hillside of rough grass littered with grey and white stones and a small smile came to her lips. There, across the hillside, and as plain as an arrow drawn in sand, was the blue and white path which led to the prickly witch.

On the brow of the hill the prickly witch observed the girl's indecision. She felt indecisive herself. Why had she run from the girl? And, if she wanted to escape from the girl, why had she left the trail of flowers? And would the girl follow the trail anyway?

The greedy girl did begin to follow the trail, which answered that question for the witch. Then the prickly witch began to feel a great excitement in herself, which made her want to run and run. She would run because she felt like running, which answered one more of her questions.

She jumped up and began to run, and then she found the answer to the last of her questions, for she was not running along the brow of the hill away from the girl, nor was she running over the brow and into a faraway valley, away from the girl. She was running instead, down the hill, weaving through the grey and white boulders, through the haze of blue and white flowers. She was running, back along her own trail, to find the smile of the greedy girl.

VALERIE'S RIB

Kym Martindale

It's cold on the crag, perched high on a hillside in North Wales on a bright autumn day. The wind carries a hint of winter. The sun has a false brightness. But there's a sweetness in being with you again. That, the cold and the anticipation of the climb we're after, make me tremble inside.

We've met with other friends for this trip. On other weekends, we've been on our own, and this is the first moment today away from the others, when we're able to pick up where we left off, able to break in our relationship once more. For over a year, we've driven up and down the country to inch up the crags and mountains of the land at least twice a month. I sometimes think we've rollercoasted too quickly, too intensely together, knowing and not knowing each other. I know how you climb, I know how you think on certain matters, I don't know how you love, cry, feel.

The first time I met you, you held me with an unblinking look at arm's length. Fresh from an over-friendly mountaineering club where everyone hugged like bears, my smile slipped as I ran face first against the granite assurance and formality you keep clamped nut-shell tight about you. It terrified me.

We're less tentative now. We've shared too many routes and nights in tents and I've formed a less scary you, a sadder you, from the rootless childhood you describe. You've been wearing that shell for very good reasons, but for so long it's grown into your skin. It still fools me. I still defer to it. But, when you're open to me like this, there's a wholeness about us. We bandy jokes. We touch carelessly, you leaning on my shoulder as we read the guidebook, and as you're not one to squander such gestures, I can't help but be moved by it.

We shiver and giggle. We lay out gear, uncoil our ropes, and pick the tools for the deed – the pieces of metal that jammed into cracks will stitch the rope to the rock and provide a life-saving pendulum should one of us fall.

I'm to lead the first pitch. You settle yourself in gloves and jacket, to belay me. I glance at you with some envy. You're always businesslike about making yourself comfortable for a belay as if you're saving the tension for the rock. Me, I can't let it go until the ropes are coiled and we're bouncing down the descent. More immediately, I envy your gloves. It's not possible to climb in gloves.

I start up the route. The rock numbs my hands instantly. The higher I go, the chillier the wind whistles. I'm about fifteen feet up when you shout, 'Do you really want to carry on? It's freezing.'

You look pinched and I realise you're right. It is too cold. Why couldn't I say it was too cold? Why was I soldiering on? Uncomfortably obvious to me is that, if I'm cold, it's because I'm soft; if you're cold, it's the weather. It's the way I am around you.

However, I scramble happily down, plucking burning-cold metal from the cracks, and we decide to go to Tremadog. The crags are more sheltered and Eric's café provides tea and toast between routes. Our faces flame up in the car after the biting wind. You drive and I sit gazing at the bright, wind-scoured hills as the sun pouring through the windows warms my lap.

When we get to Eric's, the others are already there, so it's tea and toast, and a mooch over the guidebook to choose a climb. I recall good days at Tremadog,

shooting up and down routes like monkeys, ticking
them off one by one in the guidebook – the climber's
equivalent to 'twitching'. We pick on a route and
lounge back while the others decide on theirs.

The route we picked takes us nicely to lunchtime.
We're warmed up now and at home on the rock again.
The sun is hot and we stretch like cats, a far cry from
the cold huddle of this morning. Back at Eric's, we
swap route-stories with the others and plan the
afternoon. That's when you pluck Valerie's Rib from
the guidebook.
    Valerie's Rib. We have a history, you and I and
Valerie's Rib. Earlier in the summer, we nibbled
nervously at the first pitch after it was recommended
to us by a climbing acquaintance in Eric's. Oh yes,
nice route, very pleasant, said Stella airily, standing
feet apart in wellies. A small, blonde and wiry woman,
face sharp as a blade, she swarms up much harder
graded routes than we care to dream about, and is
economical with smiles. 'She probably climbed Valerie's
Rib in those wellies,' you muttered as we sat below it,
'I've never seen her in anything else.'
    We were sitting below it because we couldn't be
sure if we'd found the right start to the route. We
dithered about, screwing up our faces and matching
rocks to diagrams, worried by the spectre of the E1
route, Valour, a grade we only aspired to, lurking ten
feet away. If we wandered on to that by mistake . . . we
shuddered. In the end, we beat a retreat, but it was
honourable; we had several other climbs notched up
and besides, it was getting on for tea-time.
    But, we're loathe to let a piece of rock give us the
slip, and when you pick it from the book, it's like a
plum, hanging ripe and ready. Bev speaks up help-
fully. She's done it and can remember where it starts,
the start being the source of our misgivings last time.
She'll come as guide but doesn't want to climb it
again. She spent a lot of time dangling off an overhang
in tears while her partner shouted at her to be sensible
and stop whining – a woman, too.
    Never mind the horror stories, we think, she'll

know the route and we climb better than Bev. It's a
selfish game sometimes.

For all that, it takes an hour to locate the start, up
and down through brambles, Bev wrinkling her nose
and ·frowning, us following and wanting her to
produce the route out of her pocket. We read the
guidebook searching for clues. We move the rocks in
our heads to fit the pictures, but they jolt back when
we look again.

'Little protection' says the guidebook. That means
no nice cracks or spikes to place the gear that links us
to the rope and the rock. That means if you fall, you
fall. And there's always the El.

We think we've found the route at last. Bev is fairly
sure that this is the overhang, with the tears and all.
I'm jittery, though not, to my surprise, as much as you.
It's so strange to see you unsure, I feel destabilised.
The nutshell is cracking.

We rope up however, and you decide to lead. It
means you'll take the brunt of the 'little protection'.
As second, I only have to follow on the rope, enjoying
the holds and the moves, loose of the fear. If I fall, I
dangle. But, we're ready; I belay uncertainly and Bev
looks on. It's down to you.

You chew the wall in your mind, facing it like a
piece of bad news. There's nothing joyful or clever in
the air anymore.

'I'm not happy about this,' your eyes scale the wall,
your heart fails it.

I grip the ropes and don't reply. I don't know what
to say, encourage you, inspire you, or share your
doubts. The issue is not getting you onto the climb,
but, how to deal with the climb in your head.

'It's the "little protection" that bothers me.' You
turn away and sit down. The gear on your harness
chinks and splays out on the rock.

'It doesn't matter, we can do something else.'

The conversation dribbles back and forth like this,
indecisive, riddled with doubt. Bev and I open bolt
holes for your escape.

'We're not even one hundred percent sure that this
is it,' I offer, 'and there is that El.'

'And you haven't been climbing for a few weeks,' adds Bev.

But, you can't let go. You shake yourself and glare at the fine, open slab. Bev gazes at the overhang and shivers.

'Mind you,' she says, 'I'm certain that's where I came off. I was hanging there long enough.'

The ghost of her misery settles on you. That decides me.

'Right,' I say, 'let's do something else.'

So we sit on the ropes and look at the guidebook again. We chew the cud over a few likely routes and we're about to pack up and go, but you think you'll have a crack after all. We return to our old stances, Bev and I, resigned to your stubborness, but pleased by it. You reach for the wall and move on to it.

It's a breathless moment; for you, from fear; for Bev, anxious with her memories; and for me, seeing you struggle with yourself like this. I feel we've reached the bare bones of you and something wakes in me. My heart wants to heal your dilemma, scoop away the fear and leave you brave and whole. In a second, I've started to love you, or feel that I could. All this blazes through me as you step back from the wall. The holds aren't there, there's no protection. Too right, I think. There's no protection at all, for either of us. Your shell is in pieces round your feet and I'm suddenly raw with emotion.

I want to hug you, but only cup my hand round your shoulder and say, 'It doesn't matter.'

Surprisingly, you grin. 'Do you want to give it a go?' you ask.

I'm pinned to the floor by this offer. I'd been concentrating so hard on your crisis, that I hadn't listened to my own eagerness, hadn't attended to the pattern of moves I'd worked out in my head which, I was sure, would dance me up the slab. But, I'm torn. I don't want to steal your lead. It's your star and my leading it would be a tarnish. Then again, you need to reclaim the climb, we both do. This might be the way.

I look at you. The skin just beneath your eyes is a delicate shell pink. 'Yeah,' I say, still unsure if this hurts or pleases you; a little of both perhaps, 'I'll give it a go.'

You prepare to belay me, methodical, without spark. I try to control my skittish feet. It's insensitive to be so eager in the face of your dismay. You're quiet, containing it, and smile at me as I step forward. I move onto the rock with sadness, excitement, blithe gaiety, and apprehension, for you, me and the climb all at once. Bev sits down to watch and I recall her presence with a shock; I'd been so involved with us.

It's not easy on the rock. The wall is deceptive and seems to push out slightly, as if to repel. My toes are on a ledge which blends eventually into the rock, just at the point when I need its security to reach for a hold. And there is no protection. I don't blame you at all for retreating; another time, I might have done. But, today I'm fearless, drunk on the confidence that's usually yours and somehow I make the moves to the overhang.

You call up your congratulations. They thrill me and sadden me. But, you'll do this one day, I tell myself, you'll have your lead. Everyone gets bad days.

The overhang is tricky. I feel Bev watching, and remember her misery here, but I've got some protection in and can check out the next move with some security. It's a bold move. Once I go, I'm committed, no going back except swiftly down. My heart starts to pump, my arms begin to ache. I've got to make the move before I tire of clinging and slither off. I take a deep breath and push up, reaching and reaching – and the hold is there. I knew it had to be, or this would be a much harder-graded route, but the relief flows in all the same. My cramped stomach eases and I move round the bulging rock to stand straight at the end of the first pitch. It's over. And I'm used up.

'Safe,' I call down.

Your face is pale in the gloomy leaves and brambles. 'Well done.'

Bev stands up to leave. The show has finished. The drama is past. You get ready to climb. I find myself thinking of Stella again, how we had to tell her last time, that we hadn't been able to find the route.

'Couldn't find it,' she exclaimed, 'but, it's that obvious nose, you can't miss it.'

I remember how this bothered you. 'Obvious nose,' you've been muttering ever since, whenever the route is mentioned, 'if it's so obvious, why didn't they call it Valerie's Nose?'

I remember too, my surprise at the depth of your rancour. You've wanted this route for a long time. Well, now we're on it and you can have the rest of it. As you come easily up the wall, I peer up at the next pitch. Nice open climbing, good angle, still not so good protection. But, I can see the line of Valour, the El. No chance of us wandering on to that. I'm drained however; the minute you get past the overhang, still quiet, still struggling to piece back your shell, I hand over.

The rest of the climb goes with smooth precision. We move happily in the sun on warm rock. You handle the lack of protection with professionalism, placing it where you can, spying likely cracks with a cool eye, neat, deft, careful. This is the you that I've always known on the rock.

On the last pitch, I have to nip behind a bush on a good thick ledge. 'Tell Stella we pissed on Valerie's Rib,' I say.

'Not quite on that nose, unfortunately,' you say.

'We could re-name it Stella's Nose,' I suggest.

We reach the top and coil the ropes. I'm still churning with a mixture of feelings. I'm pleased with myself over that first pitch, and I'm full of tenderness for you.

'Next time, you'll lead it,' I say.

'I don't know what it was,' you say, not giving too much away. Maybe you feel you've given too much already. 'Bev didn't help, going on about her trauma with the overhang.'

You are so much surer now. Leading the rest of the climb has mended the shell, and I begin to feel the hardness of it. It hurts. It blunts the edge of my tenderness. I don't want to love you, I think as you sweep up the coiled ropes and sling them round your neck. You head for the descent route, analysing the climb, reliving the details, every reach, every hold. You can even be detached about the first pitch. I don't want to love you at all. I don't want to spend time and energy battling with this outer covering, searching for cracks and digging in them to find you, and worst of all, helping you to cement them back. There would be too much pain in loving you.

We slide down the muddy path, swinging over tree roots, rocks and branches shiny with thousands of descents. I toss comments about the route into your post-mortem, moved by the curve of your shoulders and hating and hating it. The whole focus of you and I, is climbing. It's really all we know about each other. We've built our house on rock, but the ground is shifting under me. I do not want to love you, my heart screams.

But, later in the day, I watch you lead another route with Bev, and my heart changes rhythm as you appear above the tree-line, small, sure and moving with no hesitation.

PATHS

Caroline Natzler

The house stood alone in the middle of low fields, dull brick, truncated as if it had once been part of a terrace. A privet hedge enclosed it and outside hung a Bed and Breakfast sign, flapping occasionally in the gusts caused by passing lorries.

The day was warm and sunless.

A car drew up and a tall woman angled herself out, stood a moment looking up at the house. The upstairs windows were blocked with the backs of dressing table mirrors. She smoothed the pleat in her grey skirt, and hesitated.

'This O.K. love?' the taxi driver said, chewing. His hairy outdoor arm passed her a suitcase. 'That's two pound, fifty.'

She walked up the three paving stones and rang the doorbell. It shrilled far inside as if the house were empty. She stood, tall and motionless in wan clothes, and looked away over the fields, black with charred stubble, brown, parched with the long dry summer.

'Hello, dear, you must be Miss er – Mrs? Weyland!' The floral apron bounced at her in greeting, a middle aged woman with tufts of blonde hair, dark where the dye was coming out. 'Come on in – I'm Mrs Tipton.' She leant towards the suitcase. 'Oh, you'll need a man for that!' she exclaimed.

'I think I can manage, thank you,' said Miss Weyland. Her voice was like a sigh.

107

Slightly unsteady with the luggage, she followed the landlady down the hall carpet, blocks of red framing squashed flowers.

'We don't have many rooms for single ladies,' said Mrs Tipton brightly. 'Men's different if you know what I mean. So I've put you in here dear. It's really an extra sitting room. Nice and comfy.'

'Thank you,' said Miss Weyland.

She stood in the doorway looking at the chintz sofa and armchairs grouped like a family photograph around the occasional table. A gritty smell of dust agitated by recent hoovering. In front of the fireplace squatted a wooden clothes' horse, bare but for three small white towels like napkins; an old trumpet gleamed ruddy in one corner and a portable TV balanced on the window seat. Pushed against the wall was a bed with a green bedspread, beached like a boat on dry land.

'Thank you, it's fine,' she said flatly. She stood in the doorway and waited for the landlady to go.

'Supper's at six thirty – but you'll need to order it by ten thirty in the morning. Breakfast's from seven to eight. We've got a lovely set of people here at the moment,' Mrs Tipton chatted, her thumb stroking the brass door handle as she looked fondly round the room. 'Nice walks around here – you'll see we've got maps in the hall – and there's some nice little shops in the village – and the sea's not far away, only fifteen minutes by bus from the village . . . or you can always get a taxi, Tom and his son are ever so obliging . . .' She glanced at Miss Weyland and paused. 'Here for a break are you, dear?'

Miss Weyland didn't seem to hear. She lifted her suitcase onto the sofa, the veins on her hands like threads of pain.

'Thank you, Mrs Tipton, that's fine.' She looked round at her with grey eyes.

Mrs Tipton shut the door quickly, shaking her head and padded down the hall to her bubbling bright kitchen.

Miss Weyland did not open her suitcase. She left it on

108

the sofa, the tight buckle gleaming, and sat on the edge of the bed. On the mantlepiece two clocks ticked out of time like ageless insects. She moved the clothes' horse aside and looked in the mirror. A long face, intelligent bone wreathed in soft lines, almost calm. She half-smiled at herself in reassurance, the habit of women who look sideways at each other in powder room mirrors. Loosened from its clip, her hair fell brown and grey over the collar of her blouse. She walked slowly to the window, glanced in some bewilderment at the trumpet and looked away over the torn fields. And then she took from her handbag a small framed photograph, put it gently on the table; sat on the window seat, balancing a letter pad on her knee and wrote, crossed out and re-wrote, nursing the pad. Intent as a pieta.

Miss Weyland walked to the village across the fields, along tracks of stubble and cow parsley broken with the heat, dropping with platters of dry brown seeds. In the fields lay a few bright poppies like shrivelled balloons. She posted her letter.

Every day she walked the same way to the village and posted a letter.

There were whisperings at breakfast.

The room was shaded with net curtains, latticed like a confessional where only stale sins are told and forgiveness is weary.

'Yes dear.'

Couples made muted plans, their faces fixed.

Tablecloths were draped low to the ground.

'We can get a nice cup of tea there.'

Marmalade was spread thinly on toast.

'That's right.'

A knife scraped. Silence.

'Cereal or fruit juice, Miss Weyland?' The solicitous young waitress withdrew.

Miss Weyland laid her envelope beside her plate, sat erect and turned the pages of her book. No one looked at her.

109

'Difficult terrain to negotiate, those hills,' grunted a florid man in the corner, rustling his map.

His younger companion nodded, and chewed his sausage discreetly.

'A challenge.' The older man half-cleared his throat but thought better of it.

Spooning cereal, two young women with moon-cropped hair sat looking at each other. Faces burning.

'We could cycle to Newcombe. It's mostly down-hill,' murmured one.

'We'd have to come back, silly!' whispered the dark-eyed one. 'Anyway, we've been there!'

Miss Weyland glanced over at the urgency in her voice.

'That was where that stone was, the crossroads. And you said it was where women used to wait, for twenty years, for their lovers and sons to come back.'

The other woman turned her glass slowly, her eyes on her friend. Then she mouthed something which might have been, 'Would you?'

'For you? Don't be absurd!' A snagging of the breath in laughter.

The long tablecloth rumpled on the ground as if two hidden animals were nosing each other. Miss Weyland looked away again and read her book.

Mrs Tipton slithered scrapings of jam from the plates back into the pot. 'Don't know what's happened to the post, must be ten days since that young man's been,' she said to the waitress, who nodded and slid off her rings to do the washing up.

'Kevin!' Mrs Tipton shouted down to the base-ment. 'You going off to the band practice or not? You'll be late. And it was you wanted that new horn.'

Grunts and crashes. 'Kids ... !' She heaved a proud sigh.

Miss Weyland took a less direct route that morning, through sour nettles. She walked stiffly, her face rather pinched, her pale jacket flopped over one arm like a tired child. Irrigation channels of low brown water idled through the nettles and thistledown to the fields, and the sun sat steamy above her in a white sky. Clouds of small flies hung in front of her as she walked. Hardly frowning, she brushed them aside now and then with the envelope like niggling, weary thoughts.

The path went up a slight incline and along the top edge of a field where wheat was still growing high, sloping down to razed brown fields, patches of black, and carbon dark hedges. The ears of the wheat made a surface like candlewick, flesh-brown. She stopped and looked, breathed in as if to sigh, but did not.

The warm air clung. Pigeons cooed in a nearby wood, the last notes of the trill broken off, repeatedly and abruptly. Miss Weyland brushed a stray thread of hair from her forehead, put the envelope in the pocket of her jacket and walked along the track, occasionally snapping dry grass from the hedgerow.

She passed a crumpled tree trunk, where plants grew from chunks of red brown wood. Clutched her jacket to her, looked up; a cloud, a pillar of smoke fleeing over the sun, enveloping its rays, leaving the sun alone, intact as a proud red moon through the belching cobwebs of smoke. She coughed with the smell of burning, holding her bare hand to her mouth, and her eyes watered. As quickly it passed, and the sun's rays fell back and only the smell of burnt stubble was left, graining the air, something warm remembered.

She dabbed at her eyes and stood looking down at the dwindling line of fires like winking brake lights in a far field.

Jerking up from the wood two birds flapped off in opposite directions, screeching.

By the time she reached the village the sky was grey and the air stripped bare, cool. She put on her jacket, burying her hand in the pocket where the envelope was and walked steadily through streets walled with houses. Shoppers pushed past, and children on bicycles. A few chilly holiday makers clutched ice creams and laughed. Her eyes skimmed people and looked away again.

At the village green, a tatty triangle of grass and

dog mess, she passed an elderly couple on a bench. The man held a newspaper close to his face. 'Heavy-weight's second mistress,' the headline swallowed the page. 'Wife speaks'.

'I said . . .' the woman next to him chewed her words. A church bell tolled the half hour. 'I said . . .' she waited.

'What?' The newspaper scarcely stirred.

Miss Weyland's mouth crinkled slightly as she walked on to the post office.

'Not so much as a by your leave or a good-bye. No gratitude.' The woman in the queue shuddered. 'Off in London – drugs, God knows what – hasn't even told his mum his address.'

'Well, it's that generation, isn't it? Spoilt.' Her friend rooted in her bag. 'You seen those new biscuits they got in Bartons?'

Miss Weyland took a pound coin from her purse and rolled it almost tenderly between her finger tips. Then she replaced it, took out some small change and bought one stamp. She stuck it on very straight, smoothing it as if closing the eyes of someone dead.

The red pillar box sat chummy outside the post office. She held the envelope in her hand and walked stiffly past it to the ladies' toilet. A scramble of graffiti; Mandy loves Roy, Pat and Dick, ~~Mandy~~ Karen loves Roy forever.

Outside again, she lent against the wall and closed her eyes. Wisps of hair brushed her face and a breeze lifted a corner of her skirt. She opened her eyes and watched a man, his hand heavy on a pushchair.

'You mind you do, then!' He scowled down at a young woman pale with goosepimples, who gaped at him. Her heels were blood raw from her shoes. The child in the pushchair wailed and she stuck a dummy in her mouth. 'You watch it!' said the man, and left.

Miss Weyland found a litter bin on the green. Gently, as if folding a precious white dress, she tore the envelope into eight pieces, and dropped them in the bin. They made no sound.

Jacket perched on her shoulders, she walked back

briskly, looking up at a sky scurrying with cloud and sunshine. Breathing, so that her face burned. For a while a tractor whirred beside her, ploughing the stubble back into the turned earth.

In her room the sun washed shallow over the green bedspread and the trumpet glowed.

She laid her jacket on the bed, stood and considered the photograph for a moment, fingered the frame, shrugged and left it there.

A woman was crying upstairs, relentless as heartbeat.

'What's going on?' muttered Mrs Tipton as the dark-eyed young woman thundered down the stairs and crashed the front door to behind her. Mrs Tipton checked the glass in the door. The crying went on.

And, halting at first, pulling up from the deep into daylight, from Miss Weyland's room came the bellow of a trumpet.

'Well ...' Mrs Tipton shook her head and turned away.

SULPHUR

Lucy Kimbell

Tell me the story of your knees, she said to Sarah as they both lay curled in one corner of the mattress. Sarah lay wrapped round Jo, her bum fitting into the corner of the two walls and her legs bent parallel to Jo's. With her topside hand Sarah was drawing a finger line over Jo's body. In this position, she felt like a coat although one wasn't needed since it had been one of those hot days of a perverted summer: all blue and gold and no water. The window above them was open, the piece of material that acted as a curtain motionless, undisturbed by the noise that rocked in from the street: shouts, footsteps, cars being parked and being driven off.

Sarah felt like a coat that wasn't needed on such a night. Jo felt hot. She said again, tell me the story of your knees, and waited for the unfolding that would release her from this streaming body behind her.

Once, began Sarah, there were two knees, a left and a right, although they didn't perceive themselves as left and right. They were just there, inseparable. From some angles it looked as if they were trying to turn to face each other, but generally they just stared straight ahead. Some days they found themselves kneeling on a wooden bench in a cold place that was a church. The knees did not like being crushed in that way. Other times they were squashed flat against cotton along with the rest of the body: squashed breasts, squashed belly and the mound of Venus, squashed knees.

Sarah touched Jo gently and both she and Jo moved onto their knees. In the ritual of their storytelling, both had become more sensitive to such small messages. For Jo, this sharing had begun after perhaps five years and perhaps six lovers, when she found herself crying as she lay wrapped in a tall woman with brown skin and serious eyes. The woman collected her tears and poured them over her head as a libation to Venus. The woman gave her a new name and blessed each of her parts, two by two, and five by five, except where there was one.

There was one temple of Venus.

The woman's name was Sarah.

The story continued and Sarah continued telling it. Some days, she said, the knees felt whole together and other days they keenly felt the distance between them. They were similar but different. They were a pair. Some nights they slept nestled together and other nights they lay apart. Some days they were hidden together under fabric, other days hidden from each other in tunnel trousers.

When each knee was six years' old, she continued, making a total of twelve years, they fell, badly. Of course they had been crashing into things for years – bumping into chairs and walls and doors, falling onto concrete and carpet and mud. This time they fell onto pavement slabs sprinkled with glass, and in doing so, the legs twisted and brought one knee down before the other. The left knee bore the weight of the body and landed on a sharp glass edge. The right knee fell and even when still again felt the pain stored in the twist. The left knee managed to spit out the piece of glass and was dressed and healed. The right knee needed no lint decoration. It had a proud purple bruise. This was the beginning of their separation.

The night was still hot despite the cool breath of Sarah's storytelling. She paused as she and Jo leaned towards each other to kiss. Jo reached out to Sarah and followed the lines of the bones down her thighs to her knees. In the dark she could not see, but could feel, a small smoothness where the rest of the skin was dry. You're flaking, said Jo. We are wet but dry in this unknown heat. Our skins need nourishment.

Sarah nodded but her stillness was such that she felt unable to stand up to fetch the bottle of dew lotion on her table. She pressed herself back into the corner of the room in which she had folded herself earlier and felt the coldness of the walls bite into her skin. She continued.

The second thing that made the knees feel their difference was something that is not recorded on their surface. The knees were in a science lesson. All the pupils were learning about their bodies and all their knees were being used as exhibits. The teacher was passing a small wooden hammer around and was inviting the children to test his or her reflex action. These knees here, said Sarah, were two of only four knees in the class that did not both work. The left knee jerked when tapped but the right didn't.

Sarah stopped again and reached out to Jo. Their hands joined between them and as they flexed and bent their wrists, their joints cracked. Then Sarah let go, got up from the mattress and pulled away the material from the window to tie a knot in it. Jo rolled over onto her back so that the streetlight coming in the window lit up her body. Her whiteness became sulphur yellow. From her table Sarah took a lipstick, a new one with a still pointed point, and bent down by Jo's legs. I want to join the dots, she said, and on seeing Jo's teeth gleam in the yellow light, she began.

The lipstick quickly proved too unwieldy for fine designs so she went back to the table for the green eyeliner. Number one, she said, and started at one side of Jo's belly button, making a green point there. Number two, she said, and dotted a point close to it. Number three.

And so on. When she finished the area around Jo's belly, she moved up to her breasts, dotting her dots more gently here. Are you using my freckles? asked Jo.

I can't see them well but I know where they are, said Sarah, stopping her lines of dots to colour in a

116

mole on her own stomach. Returning to Jo's lower belly, she began drawing dots from her soft dark hairs outwards.

I don't have any freckles down there, said Jo. It never sees the sun.

Sarah nodded but continued.

The green dots finished, Sarah paused to survey her artistry. Jo lay still with her eyes open looking at the cool wall while Sarah moved about her.

That was the outline; now the filling in, said Sarah.

And she went back over her dots with the purple lipstick, being sure to apply it thickly and evenly. When she had finished she went to the mantelpiece and took the heavy square mirror and held it above Jo. She angled it such that the light coming in the window falling on Jo was reflected back up into the mirror. Revealing to Jo her sulphur self.

Around her bellybutton there lay a juicy-lipped kiss. She saw her heavy breasts joined by vines and she saw serpents of Venus emerging from her pubic hair.

I didn't know my tummy smiled, she said.

Then, looking up at the other woman, she reminded Sarah that she had not finished her story.

Sarah put the mirror back on the mantelpiece and joined Jo on the mattress. They sat apart leaning back on their arms with an angle betweeen them, Jo's designs, Sarah's designs, still lit from the street. Sarah started again:

The third thing happened when the knees were each seventeen, making a total of thirty-four. They found themselves weak. This had happened before but never so seriously. These brown knees that did not jerk correctly when tapped were now the focus of attention for the rest of the body. The knees kept almost collapsing each time that the eyes caught sight of another girl at school. The rest of the body was not pleased to be let down so. Well, things happened and the body found itself moving in ways it had not thought possible. Of course, the body had known, had tried other ways with other, different bodies. But this time, with this girl, for the first time, the body found itself dancing. The knees became strong again and knelt before this girl's body. The body was strong and proud.

Now Sarah halted again and moved up off her arms to turn so that she was kneeling in front of Jo. They locked eyes and then Sarah said:

I knelt forward and kissed her here.

And she knelt forward.

THE BIG HEAD

Hilary Bichovsky

Next to her on the pillow the young woman's head lay
streaked with moonlight and there was no getting
away from it – it was too big. Distantly Orion shone –
even the stars in the sword – but when she turned her
gaze to her sleeping partner those too-big features just
leapt out at her and made her feel a little sick. 'It's
because I'm used to looking at people from across the
room,' she thought. 'I'd forgotten their heads were
bigger when you got close up.' She was bathed in
sweat from the effort of not moving, not wanting to
rub against the other's skin, wanting to avoid the
other's skin. It was a beautiful night for insomnia and
her thoughts were outside the window, mainly,
sliding across the sky with the clouds. Her thoughts
inside the room were this: 'I hate people when they're
asleep, they're like animals, mouths open – don't care
even if they fart like a trumpet and the worst thing is
they care nothing about you.'

'Susan,' said the other in her sleep, reaching an
arm out, groping for a lover to hold on to. She found
Gwen's waist and got a grip on it. 'Nine, eight, seven.'

She really couldn't take much more.

'Don't leave me baby,' said her friend.

'Takes the biscuit,' thought Gwen and began to
disengage herself from the duvet, gingerly removing
her clammy buttocks from the other woman's lap.

The sleeper stretched out luxuriously in the bed and continued the star role in her melodrama. 'Why not, if that's what we want?' she announced and waited for a reply.

Gwen searched for her socks. At least now she wouldn't have to face the jokes at breakfast. At least this way the failure was made public. If they got up and breakfasted together, the assumptions would all be automatic. She fastened her watch and wondered where her earrings were. 'I can't chance turning on the light,' she thought, 'I just hope I don't wake the dog. She'll get a shock when she wakes up perhaps. But no worse than she did when she tried to kiss me.' She checked in her pockets that her doorkey and her wallet were in place and then crept stealthily, heart thumping like a thief's, towards the bedroom door. Stealing herself back again.

In the corridor the dog woke up and fixed her with its eyes, beginning to thump its tail eagerly on the ground. 'Hello sweetie,' she said, 'keep your fucking mouth shut,' and tiptoed past it to the porch. Click, click, the lock was shut and the dark blue night slipped effortlessly into her lungs. Outside again. Well out of the range of intimacy. Loneliness flushed through her like adrenalin and she pushed the pedals down.

SECOND SIGHT

Aspen

Jean hadn't given a real reading all week. It was an uncomfortable fact that her visions did dry up for long periods. She'd tried for years to grasp the combination of factors, of presence, mood, of ambience – even the weather, which might be the keys to her insights. But the fact remained that she really had no clue as to how it worked. She asked herself again how she had got into this commercial selling of her gift? After all, she wasn't obliged to, and it didn't pay all that well. Vanity! She'd had a run of insights, and it must have gone to her head. 'Well, I did give some good advice,' she thought to herself, 'and some nasty situations were avoided . . .' She looked towards the curtain which served as a door. No one had passed through it for an hour and a half. She was bored. All the customers for the last few days had been drones; no one with real spirit. Nothing for her to engage with.

The curtain moved slightly and Jean looked up. There was no one there, however, and she decided the wind must have gently rustled the fringes on the edge of the heavy burgundy cloth. Sometimes the sea breezes blew so strongly that she had a job to keep the curtain down when she was consulting, and she could see the inevitable crowd of holiday makers outside, pushing to see past the client's back. She wondered what on earth they imagined they might see at first –

she was just an ordinary middle-aged women with long fingers and a boring hair style. That was before Pat had persuaded her she needed a 'fortune teller's image'. She looked at her shawls, rings and the (far too expensive) crystal ball in centre place on the table. All unnecessary! They had nothing to do with it! But she had to admit all the glitz helped her to hide a little, and the glimpses the public were getting from behind the cloth were satisfying their expectations of a fortune teller: business had picked up.

Wait a minute! That was unmistakable . . . something was there. Jean's skin prickled, and the hairs on the back of her neck raised slightly. She was alert with heart racing and her long fingers instinctively came to rest on the underside of the crystal ball. Something was approaching her with great speed, and she closed her eyes to focus. A great blast of hate hit her and her eyes snapped open just as a man of about thirty came in. Jean was shocked by the contrast of the violence of his field and the amiable smile which clothed his face. From the agitation around him she expected him to burst in and demand her money or satisfaction of his demands, but he actually stood back and asked politely if she was open to consultation? Jean closed her eyes briefly and swathed herself in a protective aura. Then she politely asked him to sit down.

'What do you want?' he asked abruptly, 'five pounds, ten pounds? You can have what you want, I've got it!' He whisked five and ten pound notes out of his pocket and laid them on the table. Jean kept her fingers on the ball and looked straight into his eyes. She immediately saw that he had a hard thick wall of protection. With a jolt she realised that despite his open expression he was reading her every move. Fast, she wove more threads around her and struggled to concentrate within the intense heat coming from him now.

'How long do you need . . . to prepare?' he asked, in a voice at last betraying the agitation he was clearly suffering. Then he suddenly reached forward as if to touch her fingers on the ball.

'How dare you!' she flashed, her fingers pulsing

with shocks, and she saw from the way his mouth opened slightly that she had impressed upon him the distance she demanded. Settling her shoulders in a more relaxed pose, she gazed at him for a few moments. 'We can begin now,' she said.

'My name is Rod, Rod Hamilton . . . and I've lost my wife . . . well, she's not exactly my wife, we've been living together for four years. We have our own home, a nice garden, everything . . .'

'Everything?'

'Our relationship was a good one , no ties, we were both free. We'd both had other affairs, but we always came back to the original one, that was the agreement. She's just disappeared – walked out one night, and never came back. You've got to help me find her!'

'Maybe she doesn't want to be found?'

Jean felt a sudden wave of fury pass around the room, and watched disbelieving as his face remained impassive . . . not a ripple, not a muscle moved, his skin rested relaxed on his open features. This man had a gift of masks, and used it. Risking further disturbance, she decided to test how far it would go. She felt confident. She felt calm. She was sure she could handle someone so in the grip of their emotions.

'Perhaps she found that you weren't the one after all?' she went on, but she ignored the blast that hit her, easily bouncing it back across to him. 'She may have found that she loves someone else more . . .' Her voice seemed to trail off, her neck muscles went rigid. Frantically, she strove to hang on to strands of her own consciousness as her mind became filled with horrifying visions. She saw him trembling and jagged with anger, she saw him confronting a small woman. She felt murderous intent drive every muscle towards her. He was approaching the woman, who was holding out her hands to stop the attack. His hands were reaching out for her neck . . .

'What do you see? Tell me what you see!' he demanded.

Jean came back suddenly and stared at him. Nothing. No hint of emotion or trouble disturbed him. Jean gasped.

'What was it? You must tell me!' he went on, 'What . . .'

'I saw your murderous intent . . .' She gasped and again watched, incredulously, as his face showed nothing. Just an ingenuous half-smile.

'You must be mistaken. I would never hurt her. I love her.'

Jean started to contradict him, but realised that he was used to being completely believed. He looked completely honest. Then a change came over him slowly. 'The changing of a mask . . .' Jean thought, and this time unfocused her vision and allowed feelings to wash over her. She felt a little boy approaching, cute, charming, very charming, utterly beguiling, pushing out vulnerable feelings, needy feelings. She looked at him. His face hadn't changed.

'I know you saw something . . .' he said, his voice exactly the same. She realised that he used these projections completely naturally. She hadn't been prepared enough. She must work harder. She suddenly felt totally exhausted. She knew she had to distract him, and ease off the pressure.

'How long has she been gone?' she asked, but immediately knew the answer. She saw her walking out, in a blue coat. The time on the clock was half-past five, and the flip-over date on the calendar said 6th June. Two weeks ago.

'Two days,' he said, 'I spent all day yesterday crying.'

'So,' thought Jean, 'you're a liar as well!' She realised she did not like him. She didn't trust him, clearly no one could. He seemed dangerous and genuinely selfish, and she considered ending the interview then and there. However, a picture of the small woman holding out her hands to stop him would not go away . . . maybe she could help in some way? He seemed to believe in her gift absolutely, maybe she could throw him off the scent, keep him tied up in a fruitless search? He was disgusting, yet intriguing. He clearly had no gift of mind-reading, she was safe on that score.

'You're right!' she said suddenly. 'I have seen

124

something. I've seen a very small woman with dark hair . . .'

'That's her! That's Sarah!'

'And she was getting onto a boat . . .'

'That it, of course! She'll be going to her mother's. She lives in Ireland, although she's not Irish . . . I'll go there. You've answered my question!' He rose out of his seat, and again reached for his money and laid ten pounds on the table.

'There's just one more thing . . .' Jean said, 'before you go.'

'You've seen who she's with?'

'No, I would like to know her name.' Immediately, as she finished speaking, the word 'Kirsty' shot into sight.

'I've already said: Sarah.'

'If you want any more help, you will have to stop telling me lies,' she said levelly. She watched as a cheeky, beguiling grin spread across his face accompanied by feelings of irritation.

'It's alright, I won't be coming again.'

'I wish that were true,' Jean thought.

'Thanks a million for your help.'

'That's O.K.' said Jean, showing him through the curtain. After all, he wasn't to know she felt as if she had just saved a sinking ship. 'And,' she thought as she politely declined further customers from the little crowd outside, 'there's no way you are going to sink me!'

When Jean got home Pat was already preparing their evening meal. Jean slumped exhausted onto the settee.

'What on earth's wrong with you? Had a hard day at the office?' Pat teased.

'You could say that. I had a client in who was looking for someone, and he was a right head-banger.'

'How do you mean?' Pat came to sit down by her.

'He was . . . incredibly violent. Not in his manner, nothing he did. In fact he was too cool, in control of how he projected himself out. He appeared to be Mr Niceguy himself, but the feelings I was picking up were murderous.'

'As bad as that?'

'Yes, I'm not exaggerating. His girlfriend walked out on him and I don't blame her. Anyway he came to me to find out where she was, and I put him off the scent.'

'Do you know where she is?'

'I have no idea. I told him I'd seen her getting onto a boat, and he assumed she was going to her mother's in Ireland. But really I was just trying to recover from some of the blasts I'd got from him. I'm used to reflecting back people's feelings ... I was a social worker for too long to want to know about them more than superficially. But he volleyed them straight back a hundred times harder, and it rather knocked me off balance. I just wanted to get rid of him so I could get home and figure out what I was going to do next time he came.'

'Next time?'

'Oh yes, he's bound to be back. He believes in my gift absolutely.'

'You could just refuse to see him of course.'

'I can't do that – the girl's in danger.'

'What was that you said earlier ... about being a social worker for too long?'

Jean sighed. 'The trouble is I can't help getting involved this time. I'm getting the messages whether I want them or not. I've got to find her and warn her what danger she's in. The problem is, there's only one person who can help me to find her, and that's him!'

Jean spent several days away from her seafront booth. She needed to rest and think. She meditated. She considered ways of strengthening her shields and screens and practised them, but she knew she couldn't test them out until she saw him again. Nevertheless she wanted a wall as strong as his, and masks as good too. He'd known when she saw, and she needed to cover that. She needed skills she'd never tested before. When she finally went back to work her adrenaline buzzed. She saw several clients moved by pure curiosity, with very little of interest to her and gradually she started to feel flat and irritable. Maybe

Pat was right: it was none of her business and he wasn't coming back. Idly, she began calling him, focusing on the visions she had had before. Once or twice she practised the weaving of her protection, thicker and thicker, stronger and stronger, and filled it with confusing colours and emotions. But the effort of this wore her out. She needed to preserve her energy and stay calm. When he did finally appear, it was quite an anti-climax:

'I've returned, as you see,' he stated flatly. There was none of the drama of his previous entrance, no forewarning. He seemed worn down and depressed, but not angry. 'I didn't find her. Her mother said she hadn't been there but I didn't believe her. I think she'd been and left. I need your help again.'

This time her elaborate mental preparations during his speech seemed superfluous and unreal. But she reminded herself she might need them at any time even though he didn't seem to suspect her of deceiving him

'O.K. I need you to tell me about her . . . Kirsty. It's not so much the verbal information I want, but as you speak you will be thinking of her. I need nudges from the subconscious as well as the conscious. Don't interrupt me, just talk.'

He looked vaguely startled when Jean used Kirsty's name, but Rod did as he was told. He didn't even scan Jean's face, as he had done so keenly before. He focused on her hands resting lightly under the ball, and gradually his random anguished questions and demonstrations came round to the beginning of their relationship, and he took it from there. Jean allowed his feelings in. She was struck by the strong feelings of possessiveness and the almost total lack of love. It seemed as if Kirsty was his symbol, the means to show the world he was worth something. He idealised her and hated her. It seemed she had tried to leave him before, and Jean saw a sister involved, a tired-looking woman with glasses, and children, there were children all around. There was another woman too . . . Jean couldn't quite grasp it. There was something about water, not getting on a boat, though. It was surfing, windsurfing, laughing, crying with the pleasure, speeding through the water like a bird. She came round suddenly. Rod was questioning her.

'Well, have you got anything?'

'Tell me about the people she knows, and about her family.'

Rod obligingly ambled through a few people but there was no mention of the windsurfing. However he did talk about a fitness club in the city she went to with a colleague at work, and occasional weekends away, but Jean got no response in her mind to this, and she began to suspect that there were things Kirsty kept from him. Then he began to talk about sex. One of the reasons Jean hated sessions with men was that so many of them wanted to tell her about their exploits and ask her what she could see. She began to use her usual defence tools: 'I see a woman aching with frustration, and another experiencing feelings of extreme boredom . . .' when she realised it was not aching boredom Kirsty was feeling, but blissful responses. She looked disbelievingly at the specimen in front of her. Could it be that sex had been the reason Kirsty had stayed with someone so obviously lacking in the personal qualities a woman needed? She unfocused again, and was whirled round by feelings of bliss, and love. Heady, wet feelings. Just a minute! That was it, she was wet all over, she was in the sea. The windsurfer was the source of her bliss!

Jean pulled herself round. Rod was still droning on. Heavy blue clouds of depression hung round him. Jean was glad she'd made her screen so strong. She needed to think. She needed to give him something plausible that would keep him away for a day or two. 'You mentioned her brother has something to do with cars – a salesman? I see a red car travelling at great speed . . .'

His sudden eagerness nearly toppled her off her seat.

'But I don't know when,' she continued quickly, 'and, I have to say there's someone else with Kirsty . . .'

'Who is it? Is it a man or a woman? Tell me!'

'It's difficult to say if it's a boy or a girl, but a teenager I would say, around sixteen.'

'Don't you know where they were going, anything?'

'I think they're travelling north at great speed, or have been. Oh, and Kirsty has changed her hairstyle . . . it's short now.'

This information was met with a slight opening of the jaw, and a shock wave of disbelief and anger. Jean was again impressed by his calm exterior. She was glad her barriers were serving her so well.

'You wouldn't be winding me up, would you?' he asked suddenly, and the surprise certainly jolted Jean. But she unfocused again and felt the strong waves of paranoia which were enveloping him: he did not truly suspect her. But for how long?

Jean was almost laughing with relief when she fell through her door that night. She knew she hadn't really any reason to be complacent, but she had a lead. Pat was worried. She knew when Jean had a bee in her bonnet she very rarely let it go. And Jean hadn't been well, she'd had to retire on a disability pension because of her worsening arthritis. The hay fever season was coming up and it always punished her harshly. She still had her car but long journeys were out of the question, yet here she was talking about investigating the windsurfing clubs. Pat suddenly had a horrible feeling she was going to be roped into something she didn't fancy.

'Oh go on, you've got a gorgeous figure!'

'I'm not interested in trying windsurfing just to show off my figure!'

'But you look stunning in a swim suit, why don't you give me a treat?'

'I'm too old for this detective lark . . .'

'You're too old to sit in front of a computer all day you mean. When did you last do something really physical?'

'You should know!'

'That's how I know you'll be great at windsurfing.'

Several weeks later Pat had received several expensive lessons from the only woman windsurfing instructor within a fifty-mile radius, and she and Jean were sharing coffee with two friends, Sue and Rachel, on the dock after a lesson.

'What's it like then?' Rachel was asking, looking dubiously at the murky water. 'That water looks like a mixture between petrol and blue-green algae.'

'And tastes like three-week old washing up water,' added Pat. 'Actually it's the most exciting thing I've ever done in my life . . .'

'Well, thanks a lot!' Jean complained.

'Put it like this,' said Pat, 'I've hardly been able to walk, let alone do anything else since the day I started — my muscles ache like fury!'

'We make a grand pair!' said Jean, whose pains had been tedious.

'Actually, Ruby did warn me . . .'

'Ruby?' asked Sue.

'The instructor, and what a dyke!' The four women's eyes glanced gleefully from one to the other, and they all sat a little further forward.

'She doesn't half think a lot of herself as well!' went on Pat. 'When she's not windsurfing, she works out at a club. And when she's not doing either of those, she goes along to the Magnum and flexes her muscles at the bar for the girls.'

'No!' Rachel exclaimed. 'I wouldn't mind seeing what goes on at the Magnum these days. Why don't we go down there one night?'

'But there was no mention of Kirsty,' Jean added sadly, 'and I was so sure . . .'

'She may yet surface . . . ah, sorry, I didn't mean it to be a joke! She might still appear. Tell you what, there's a club expedition to Combe, to try some sea surfing, she might come along to that as it's quite far away. Why don't we all go?'

Jean was furious to find she was too laid up to join the windsurfing weekend. She couldn't stop worrying about Kirsty. It was alright for the others to treat it as a holiday and a joke, but they hadn't felt that beast's fury, or his persistence. She was convinced Kirsty's welfare depended on her, and she was gritty and

130

anxious as she said goodbye to Pat and the others. She made Pat promise to ring as soon as she could.

Which Pat faithfully did. 'There is someone with dark hair, and a bad case of the hots for Ruby,' Pat reported after the first surf, 'but she calls herself Jackie.'

'She could be using another name!' Jean retorted. 'Ask her, ask her if she's called Kirsty!'

'I can't just go up to someone I've hardly met and do that! Anyway, even if it is her, she's a perfect right to her privacy. He hasn't found her yet – perhaps he never will?'

Jean felt a foreboding. 'You must ask her. You must tell her she's in danger.'

'I don't think this is the best way to do it Jean. It's none of our business, really. Anyway, she looks to be in heaven with Ms Muscles – why should we spoil that? It sounds from what you've said as if she's had a hell of a time with that man.'

'Pat, please, you know if I was there I'd do it myself. You must get her to come and see me, at least ring me, please!'

The call ended on an acrimonious note; Jean fraught with anxiety and frustration, Pat torn between the laid-back atmosphere of the holiday and the strain in Jean's voice.

'Jean's not often completely wrong, you know.' Rachel said over drinks that evening. 'She and I go back a long way, and some uncanny things have happened . . .'

'But what am I supposed to do?' replied Pat despondently. 'Why didn't I fall in love with a cabaret singer or a beautician?'

'Because she saw you coming!' quipped Sue and they all laughed. Ruby and Kirsty walked in. Kirsty looked as if there was no one in the whole world for her except Ruby. But Ruby, who was walking slightly ahead, saw the merry bunch of lesbians and strode over to them.

'Mind if we join this joyous throng?' she asked easily, and took the spare chair. Sue got up quickly and fetched another for Kirsty, who had coloured slightly and was standing awkwardly at the edge of the group. Kirsty sat down self-consciously, and watched Ruby silently. Ruby, however, was in an expansive mood.

'You did really well today, Pat.'

'You mean I spent nearly as much time on the board as I did under the water this time?' Pat laughed. 'I seem to have finally got the knack of lifting the sail out of the water with that slight twist you've been trying to teach me.'

'Yes, if you haven't got the muscles, you've got to have the knack!' Ruby added, and Rachel and Sue burst out laughing.

'Can we quote you on that?'

Ruby smiled. She didn't know where these women had come from, but she was relieved they were there. Things seemed to have got a bit intense with her other pupil. 'Lighten up, I do have some obligations towards my other pupils you know,' she'd said in her room before they went down to the bar. Kirsty could see where Ruby's obligations were taking her. She'd noticed Pat was on her own, and Ruby was getting interested.

'No, I mean you actually got sailing this time,' Ruby went on.

'Yes, that speck you could see panicking on the horizon was really me. I got back on after my fiftieth ducking, and after a few hair-raising minutes while the boom tried to knock me off again, the wind suddenly caught the sail and I was whooshing out to sea. I was completely elated until I suddenly realised I was two miles off shore. Then I panicked and tried like fury to get back again!'

Everyone laughed. Everyone except Kirsty. Pat tried to draw her into the conversation. 'How long have you been learning, Jackie?' she asked Kirsty, and when Kirsty didn't answer and didn't look up, a feeling of unease spread through the group. 'She doesn't recognise that name,' thought Pat, 'It must be her . . .'

'Jackie! Ruby touched her knee and Kirsty looked

up at her. Such sadness. Such loss. Women really shouldn't put all their eggs in another woman's basket until they were sure the other woman wanted to carry them, reflected Pat.

'Did you find it difficult when you were first learning?' Pat asked her. Kirsty looked hard at Ruby.

'I was getting good instruction at the time!' she snapped and got up suddenly, walking quickly to the toilets. Everyone squirmed slightly and Ruby shrugged.

'She does wear her heart on her sleeve, that kid.'

Pat got up and followed Kirsty. She found her standing with her hands in a sink of water, and when Pat came in she began splashing her face.

'Jackie . . .' Pat started in a kind voice, 'is, is your name really Kirsty?'

Kirsty went white and looked at Pat.

'Why should it be?'

'I know someone who's met Rod.'

Kirsty went even whiter, and her lip trembled. 'He doesn't know I'm here, does he?'

'No. Kirsty? It is Kirsty, isn't it? He's looking for you . . .'

'He mustn't find me here!' Kirsty burst out wildly. 'He'd be crushed if he knew I'd left him for a woman!'

'My friend seems to think you're in some danger from him.'

'In danger? From Rod? You must be joking! He would never hurt me! Not like I've hurt him. I must be a complete fool to leave someone who took care of me the way he did. But I couldn't seem to help myself. Anyway, who is your friend? How does she know Rod?'

'He went to her for help, to find you. She tried to put him off the scent. He went over to Ireland to see if you were at your mother's, and the last time she saw him he was going to go north.'

'He went across the sea to my mother's? He's terrified of the sea. He always said nothing could ever get him on a boat again, he's really terrified. It's a phobia he's had since he was a little boy . . .' Pat heard the tone of voice which had gone soft and thoughtful.

'He's also carsick, completely travelsick ... Who is your friend anyway? Why are you involved?'

'My friend is a ... clairvoyant ...'

'A clairvoyant! He went to a clairvoyant to find me ...'

Pat sensed this was not going the way Jean had imagined. She tried once more to impress upon Kirsty the situation as Jean saw it. 'Yes, she is a clairvoyant, and she felt really that you are in great danger. Rod is murderously angry, not hurt, and she thinks he will take it out on you!'

'How can she know that! I've known him for four years. He's never hurt a fly. He's certainly loved me better than that bitch out there. You mind your own business, and get back to her, seeing as you're next on the menu!' And with that Kirsty stalked out showering water from her hands over Pat's feet as she pushed past her.

'What a mess! Pat thought, as she walked resignedly back to the others.

Jean cursed her disability which had prevented her doing the work herself. She was sure she could have managed it differently, and could have convinced Kirsty. It was no use Pat saying you couldn't live people's lives for them: when you saw danger threatening, it was your duty to try to prevent it. Jean worried and fretted as she went to work every day, but Rod didn't appear. She concentrated, meditated, relaxed, but nothing came through. She read all the papers but there was never any report of Kirsty.

For months Pat tried to get her off the subject, but it was like trying to get a crab off your finger: the more she tried to pull, the more it hurt her. She'd been through similar periods when Jean had been working for the Social Services, and she knew it was nearly impossible to get Jean to give up.

Nothing was resolved until one night in the Magnum, when who should come walking through the door but Kirsty – with another woman! When she saw Pat, she came straight over.

'I feel I owe you an explanation ...' she said.

'No,' said Pat, 'it's nothing to do with me. This is Jean, by the way.'

Kirsty looked at her. 'Are you the friend Pat mentioned, who's a clairvoyant?' she asked.

'Yes.' Jean said with concern. 'What happened? I saw him coming towards you as if to strangle you.'

Kirsty looked stunned. Then she smiled: 'But you didn't see what happened next. You missed the best bit, I'm afraid!' She turned to the women next to her: 'This is Alison. She's my self-defence instructor. We've done lots of work on what to do if someone comes at you like that. You see you have to use their own force against them. You knock the inside of their elbow with one hand, and simultaneously lift their other elbow. Their own force sends them sideways, and then you can kick them where it hurts and get away.'

Jean sighed with relief: 'I think I'll retire, now!' she said.

'You haven't got any more jobs for me then?' Pat asked smiling.

Jean laughed: 'Not as far as I can see!'

RED

J. E. Hardy

The high dog-days of summer, when leaves creak, crying for rain, and the house smells of burnt lawn. Each day I open windows and doors, their opening being the only draught I can create. Once they are open nothing moves. Even dust and motes have sunk into lassitude. In the mornings, early mornings, I too wake creaking for water, fruit juice, anything. Through the leaded windows the sky is already gleefully, malignantly bright. And each morning I turn over, screwing the damp sari that is my sheet tighter around me. I turn away from the light, disappointed that my dreams of growlers, of waterfalls, of rainbows are illusions. Before I sleep again I count the beads of sweat on my lip.

Old Cotswold houses have small windows and flag-stoned floors. Cotswold mansions have these and warrens of corridors, unlit by natural light. The walls of these corridors are white, cold, damp-feeling. This summer, this elevated, heat-pumping summer, I press my body against these walls each morning as I make my way to the kitchen to slake my thirst. The first thrill-chill is painful, makes my face, breasts, stomach ache. But as the wall bleeds away the pent-up night-heat of my body the pain recedes and I long to stay spread-eagled against these walls for all time.

The floor of the vast kitchen is often a mosaic, a carpet

of animal fur, heaving slowly, arhythmically with the sighs of cats and dogs spread on the cold stone floor. As I open the latch-door they barely move. The dogs raise their heads enquiringly and slowly lower them, their eyes following me to the sink, where I gulp glass after glass of water. When I open the kitchen door, open it onto a vista of soft, singed hills and wilting trees, the dogs raise their heads once more, eyebrows twitching as they look from me to the freedom of limitless land. They sigh and shuffle to another, cooler flagstone.

Today the fire of the sun has baked the air until it hangs in fields, like cigarette smoke in a closed room. Already the vest I am wearing is limp and creased, the crutch of my shorts damp and irritating. Earlier I lay in a tepid bath for an hour, lowering my temperature, yet still my hair is sticking to me, wet and ropey. Nothing dries, nothing moistens. Now the dogs must walk and I take them along a clay track, hard as rock and dusty as a chalk pit. I walk in the shadow of the trees lining the path, ignoring the trickles of sweat on my spine. The oldest dog stumbles and I turn back, my mind empty of thought, my shins light with clay dust. As I push open the back door the cat drawls a cracked miaou. I have no idea what to do with him, how to make his life easier. I stroke him and my hand comes away plastered with hairs. Enervated, I lean against the table and realise that the clock is telling me that I should eat. The doorbell clangs, its chiming warped.

Aware of the dark patches on the denim of my shorts, I pull open the oak door, which is hidden behind long, lined curtains.
   'Yes?'
   She is wearing a peppermint, white and bruise-yellow cotton dress, her blond hair stark, static, electric in the sunlight.
   'Can I help you?' I croak, my soft palate razor-sharp. I realise I have made a mistake: that is not what you say to people who knock at your door. I shake my desiccated head.

'Is Mr Rivers in?' Her voice is wet, the words sound as if they have been licked.

'No, he's not. He's away on holiday.'

'Oh. He asked us to come round and make some sketches today.'

'Sketches?' I have forgotten what the word means in my stupor.

'I'm from Gullitch and Mather, the architects.'

'Oh, oh yes.' I run a finger over my upper lip. 'Yes, I'd forgotten. Please come in.'

'Thank you.'

In the kiln that is my skull I grope for the image of the calendar hanging in the kitchen and find that it is indeed today that I was to expect someone. I stand aside and she brushes past me, the blue blast of her cooling the air. 'Um, yes. Mr Rivers told me that you'd be coming. I'm looking after the house and animals for him.'

'I see. Well, hello. My name's Red.' She holds out her hand and I wipe my sweat on her palm in shaking it.

'Red?' I ask blankly.

'Yes.'

'Oh. I'm Ellen.' Suddenly the hallway seems cramped, dark, oppressive. I throw the curtains aside. 'What do you need to do?'

She puts the files she carries on the oak table in the dining room and glances around. 'Mr Rivers wants the barn attached to the house converted into two flats. I've come to make some measurements and to do some preliminary sketching. I really need to see the whole house and grounds so that any changes I suggest will be in harmony with what's already here.'

I watch her face as she speaks and marvel at her composure, her assurance, her dryness. 'Would you like me to show you around?'

'Yes, that would be easiest. Could we start at the top and work down?'

'Fine. Follow me.'

As I climb the stairs I am aware of my clay-stained calves, of the patch between my shoulder blades, as she rustles in her cotton behind me. I lead her from

138

room to room, under the eaves, then down to the first floor and walk its length, stopping at bedrooms, bathrooms, the study — all looking out over the deflated, parched landscape. Life has oozed away even from the honey-stone of the house and gardens. In each room Red draws hasty lines on the damp, slightly wrinkled pad in her hands, her head snapping this way and that as she looks down perspectives.

'Some house,' she mutters as we go down to the ground floor once more.

'Yeah. Here's the library.' I open the door to the book-lined room, cooler than the rest with the shutters closed against the colour-fading sun.

'Good God, it's enormous.' Red wanders around the room, the only splash of colour in the gloom, reading titles and touching the books. 'It must run the length of the west wing.' She begins to draw again, smiling when she finishes.

I show her the dining room, the music room, another lounge, the kitchen, and in the light from a window I see that she has begun to sweat. Nothing but a sheen at her temple.

'Do you want to see the grounds?' I ask, desperate now for a drink.

'Yes, if I may.' She licks her full lips. 'Could I have some water?'

'I was thinking of having a beer. Would you like one?'

'Yes please.'

Holding the sweat-beaded glasses we walk out into the wavering garden. It is mid-day and the malicious light I turned my back on this morning has become a horizontal fireball stretching to infinity.

'Christ it's hot.' As I watch beads of sweat form on the backs of my hands.

'I'm surprised you feel it you're so tanned.' Red looks at the skin on my bare shoulders and licks a line of beer froth from her lips.

'In this weather it's difficult not to be. I wish it would rain.' I look up into the limitless, aluminium sky to break away from her grey eyes.

'I imagine it would be a cloud of steam if it did.'

And Red looks up too, brushing me as she turns to scan the skyline. A dog walks out and flops in the shadow of a fading rosebush, its tongue lolling. As we watch it topples over on its side and stretches its long, Lurcher body.

'We'd better make this quick or I'll turn to ashes.' Red's voice, I now realise, has a strange, alien lilt to it. Even she, the ice princess, has begun to melt.

'OK, follow me.' I lead her around the grounds and we kick up a fine dust as we cross the lawns. I feel it settling on me, in my still-damp hair, on my absorbent skin. I show her the stables, the outhouses, and finally the unnatural blue rectangle, hidden by a dry stone wall, which is the pool. Against the muted, almost lifeless Cotswold palette of honey tones and half-tones the water looks absurd, obscene. It ripples and glitters, the only moving body in view.

'Do you use it?' Her voice cracks a little.

'Yes. All the time now. It's the only way of getting cool.'

'Yes, it must be.' She sounds hungry. 'Well, I'd better do what I came to do and look at the barn, make measurements of it.'

The dog trails behind us as we walk to the barn, its paws dragging, its tongue dripping. I pull the slatted door along its rollers and motion for Red to follow me. Looking around she laughs for the first time.

'This is amazing.' She laughs again.

'Yes, I suppose it is. I've got used to it I suppose. But it is extraordinary.' I look around at the glass cases and stands, all filled with wooden models of ships. In the beams of sunlight filtering through the shrinking rafters it seems a flotilla, an armada is sailing across the vast stone floor. I switch on the lights and as the overhead spots flicker in sequence, over and over, the ships appear to bob up and down on a flowing sea.

Red walks between them, appearing to crest the waves, a giant bowsprit maiden cleaving the fleet. She is more animated than I have yet seen her, has burst into life.

'What's he going to do with all this? When the conversion starts?'

'He's donating it to a maritime museum. Apparently it's the largest private collection in the world.'

'That's my favourite,' she says, pointing to a tall-ship, black and gold, festooned with rigging, its lines and curves in perfect harmony. She touches the yard arm, runs her fingers along it, trails them across the bow. 'Beautiful.'

'I'll leave you to it then. Why don't you come to the pool when you're finished? I'll wait there.'

'I'd like that. Thank you. I shan't be long.'

I leave her amongst the hulls and masts, smiling still.

Each day in the early afternoon I lie here, at the edge of the pool, a hand dangling in the water, a sheaf of blank paper in front of me. I am shielded by the high stone wall; sound disappears and the light intensifies. Each afternoon of this summer the day holds its breath, the stillness vibrates, rumbles a little, as if a cataclysmic storm will break over us. But nothing happens.

Today I must have fallen asleep, must have slept through the growling hour, for Red is now sitting in one of the old cane chairs in the shade of a thatched roof, writing and drawing. She does not notice that my eyes have opened and over the brown, downy horizon of my arm I study her. When she arrived here this morning she was a cool, angular intrusion into my day. Crisp, ironed, composed. Now she has changed; strangely she is browner than before, her hair a warmer blonde, her eyes a different grey. She throws down the pad, stretching, and I use the cracking of the chair to feign waking.

'Have you finished?' I ask, nodding at the papers.

'Yes, I've done all I can do. I've tried somehow to work in an atrium so that light will filter down into an enclosed courtyard in the centre. Atriums were a feature of Roman domestic architecture, and I think they're beautiful.' Red fans herself with a book, then lets it fall into her lap. 'God it's hot.'

'Do you have to go back to the office now? I mean,

why don't you have a swim or something if you've got time?'

'No I don't have to go back. I'm finished for the day.'

'Well, if you want to, I've brought down a swim suit and towel for you.'

'You don't mind?'

'No, not at all.'

'Thanks.' Red stands, pulls the dress over her head and drops it in the chair. Beneath it she is naked and I cannot look away from her.

'Do you mind if I swim like this? I don't like swimming suits.'

'Well, no one else can see you.'

I watch her as she dives in, unmindful of the spatters of freezing water that shower me. From the protection of my arm's shadow I follow her with my eyes. After a while she swims over to me and rests, her back turned to me, her arms flat on the tiled edge as her feet kick lazily.

'So what about you?' Red asks. 'Do you have to get to the office this afternoon?'

I watch her profile as webs of reflected light skim over the contours of her face. 'No, I don't.'

'What do you do that you don't have to go into an office?'

'I'm a writer.' The present aridity of the words, the stack of blank paper in front of me forces me onto my back to stare at nothing.

'What do you write?'

'When I need money I write articles and features, when I feel like being poor, I try to write novels.'

'Are they any good?'

'I think so.'

'What are they about?'

'About?' I feel my face moving through shades of colour as the sun bakes it. 'What are they about?' I echo. 'Women.'

'What about women?' Red turns in the turquoise water, rests her elbows on the pool's edge and looks at me.

'Everything. Everything I know.'

142

She kicks away and splashes through the length of the pool. I turn once more so I can watch her as she climbs out. She lays her towel next to mine and flops onto it, still dripping, her hair, dark blonde now, plastered to her skull. Her splayed elbow touches mine and a silence stretches like warm elastic between us.

'So why Roman architecture?' I ask sleepily.

'Because they were the first to separate function from decoration, the first to enable themselves to do that, in the Tabularium in Rome.' She raises herself on her elbows and looks down at me, seems to loom over me, her eyes smiling. 'And there's the Pantheon, built nearly two thousand years ago, based on a perfect sphere, the simplest, most satisfying of objects. You see, they took Greek architecture – which was extrovert, tectonic – and turned it inside out, inverted it. Roman architecture is inverted, plastic, if you like. Look at colonnades – the mirror image, the reverse of Greek functionalism. Beautiful.' She looks away from me, frowning a little. 'The Pantheon was a beautiful building,' Red says wistfully. 'Awesome.'

'So why did it change? Architecture? Ways of building?'

'Because people learn, each civilization enables the next.' She is looking at me again and I am left paralysed at the end of her stare. 'Do you enable others when you write? Do you educate them? Lead them, draw them along?'

The asthmatic buzz of a distant car grows and fades. The ancient oak tree cracks restlessly behind the wall, desperate for the rains to come, feeling cheated by the endless, unfulfilled promises of storms.

'I don't know. I don't educate, I don't want to.' I swallow and my throat clicks, machine-like. I am overwhelmed by the heat, by the responsibility of this. 'I write of possibilities. Of the endless possibilities of every situation. Of the choices women can make.'

'Ah,' Red sighs. 'The Teutonic touch of death that was determinism didn't last then? I knew it wouldn't. How could it? For, as you say, there is always the spectrum of possibility.'

143

The water highlights the runnels of sweat inching down her skin as her tanned hand reaches out and touches my face, turning it towards her. And as she kisses me I feel my diaphragm freeze and then flux. Red strokes my face, my neck, my shoulders, leans away from me, enables me to choose. We look at each other across the ages and smile.

I pull her towards me and a film of sweat slips under my fingers as I caress her back, feel the heat of it pounding on my fingertips. Our bodies meet along their length as the world that is the stone wall, the fraying chairs, the moving water flies away and all I see is the violent red of my eyelids. Her mouth tastes untainted, tastes of pungent honey and sharp milk. Her full, red smudged lips move away, move to my shoulders, move across them. Her tanned, glistening hands slide down, over my now-tight nipples, over the wet washboard of my stomach. I wrap my legs around her, pull her as close as I am able and another world opens for me to replace the one that has fled. As she traces the lines of my thighs my mind fills with images of marbled rooms and columns, of olives and dust. I lick her breasts, lick away the clear sweat that has gathered between them and the sound of chariot wheels crosses between us. As I unfold her the cadence of her deep, velvet-like breathing becomes that of faint bellows heating a furnace, the clash of metal on metal ringing in the distance. Our hands, mouths and limbs slide under the sun until this new world plays itself out, until we have each felt the other fold in and gather together once more.

I find myself lying by the pool and the mad turquoise of the water shocks me. Red and I smile, and she stands, pulls me to my feet and leads me into the water. Again she kisses me, ripples fanning out around us as her hands slip between my legs.

The day's change into night passes unnoticed as we leave the pool for the dim, cool confines of a bedroom. The wine and fruit we take with us slowly disappear as the light flickers through the diamond leaded windows. Each time we look around it is darker, and finally, when there are only vermillion streaks left on the skyline, touching the horizon, we begin to dress. I watch Red as she slips on a t-shirt, knowing each line, curve, promise of the body she covers.

'Can we go to the barn again? I'd like to see it once more.'

'Yes of course.'

In the kitchen, cooler now, the cats and dogs yawn in greeting. They have slept through this day, as they never have before, leaving me undisturbed. I feed them, stroke them, thank them, and Red and I go out into the night. The barn fascinates her, draws her in, and once more she walks between the ships, pointing with child-like delight. She comes to stand by me, holds my hand loosely as she watches the miniature armada float in the lights.

'I shall never forget this,' she murmurs and kisses my hand. 'Thank you.'

We walk across the patchy grass to the house, reluctant to leave the mint-green air of the night, yet aware always of the well of desire brimming between us. As that well spills over we slip through the house and I fill a bath. But soon the washing is undone as I taste the honey and milk of her yet again and our now-tired bodies ruck the sheets.

I wake, as always, at dawn, from a tangle of dreams. My sleep has been filled with arches and armour, with clay and bowls, with shouts and silences. In the strangely grey light I see Red is dressed. An unusual sound lies between us and I hesitate to speak. It is rain, spattering the windows, tapping on leaves, making the pool jump.

'What are you doing?' I ask.

'I have to go now. I have to get back.' Red stands and smoothes her dress.

'But it's so early.'

'I know, but I have to leave.' Red smiles and comes to sit by me, brushes the damp hair from my forehead. 'Goodbye.'

'But.' I hold the hand that has touched me. 'When will I see you? How will I speak to you?'

145

Red laughs and kisses my troubled lips. 'I can always find you, now I know where you are. I can always find you.' She stands, looks around the room and smiles. 'Always.'

And she leaves me to my dreams, to the other world she has shown me.

It is the telephone by the bed that wakes me, and the sound brings the dogs bounding up the stairs to flop on my feet, panting and hairy. I have slept again since Red left, hours before, sleeping to try to recapture the taste and smell of her. I grope for the phone and realise it is still raining. 'Yes?' I mumble.

'Good morning. This is Miss Mather, from the architects' office.'

'Yes?'

'I'm calling to apologise for not being able to come over yesterday as arranged. I tried ringing all day, but no one answered. I wonder if it would be possible to arrange another appointment?'

I watch the rivulets of rain fragmenting the trees on the hills. 'Can I call you back?'

'Of course, whenever suits you. Goodbye.'

Still I watch the rain fall as the telephone crackles. But nothing happens.

ANY PORT IN A STORM*

Maro Green

O Rose, thou art sick!
The invisible worm
That flies in the night,
In the howling storm,

Has found out thy bed
Of crimson joy,
And his dark secret love
Does thy life destroy.

William Blake,
written as grafitto
on the wall of an
underground station, 1991

Jean. You poor beautiful imprudential woman! It's Thursday – the small hours.

I'm writing to you, darling, since I can't be with you. It's taken it out of me going to the hospital every day in the snow and the bombs and then bumping into her when I get there, and girding my bones to be polite. In all honesty, I don't think I could keep it up – my umph, don't you know, but the flesh isn't willing.

I've bought a bottle of retzina specially for tonight.

147

Sainsbury's do it now for only £2.38. Some olives and peter bread for you even though I can't abide them. It's to remind us of that Greek holiday we never had.

These last few days, I've been dead tired. I haven't known how I was going to put one foot in front of the other. My eyes still itch from the last anaesthetic. They don't tell you what you're in for, do they? If they did, we wouldn't have the heart to go on, would we? I've got to have the other leg done. I haven't told anyone else, Jean. I've been kidding myself it would be all right but it hurts. I tried to put my leg right out of my mind but I went to see my lovely surgeon last week, Mr Rahman. 'It must ache,' he said. 'It does ache,' I said. Why haven't I been able to face up to it – these last nine months it's ached. 'You're not a complainer,' he told me. 'No,' I told him, 'but it aches.' 'I'm afraid it's deteriorated.' Well, I knew that. It broke me up, but I didn't cry. 'I want to do some tests, Lily.' He always called me Lily from the word go. It's my name. After the flower. 'It may mean a second operation,' he said. 'Oh,' I said. He's fond of me, I can tell that. I wanted a bit of kindness. Well, the results of the tests came through this morning. I've got to have it done or they'll amputate. It never rains but it pours. But I told him, I said 'I've got this friend, my very beloved friend, and she's in a spot of trouble, and I have to get her through it before I can even entertain this other thing.'

Stinny yas mas – cheers! You can knock back retzina and not feel a thing. It doesn't affect me because I don't like the taste.

What a dance we've led each other, Jean! I'd love a fag. Our generation smoked, didn't we? 'Passing Cloud', do you remember? You like me were often glimpsed through a cloud of smoke. When you first told me you were going to die – just before you got involved with her – that it was cancer, I was livid. I wanted to grab the front of your pyjamas and shove you in the chest. I shouldn't have lost my temper, but I did. Yet I said to

148

God – not that I believe in him – 'You let Jean live, and I won't have another puff from now on' and I haven't. But I still smoke inside – it's like riding a bicycle – you never forget the taste.

One's mind plays funny tricks on you, doesn't it? I can remember that time – it's so vivid – that time you pushed me under a bus. It was just after the war, wasn't it? Nylons were still on rations so we had baths with our legs cocked over the side not to wash off the brown stain and the seams we'd drawn with eyebrow pencil. We were quarrelling. I don't know about what – oh yes, but it doesn't matter now. We won't go into that now. And we were walking along by Russell Court. 'I'm going to push you under this bus,' you said and you did! It was a 68. Sometimes I think that's all we have done – quarrel – until something tender floods back.

What about the time we hadn't a penny in the world except a pound so we went down the fish shop and when we got there we'd lost it!

Remember when we first met? When I was recruited for the SOE in the back room of that sweet-shop off Crucifix Lane by that upper-class thug, Alistair McDonald. You were there and in all that poverty just like there is today. You taught me the codes. You'd shout and scream at my deciphering but you admired me. It's a curious thing to say but no one – no other woman that is – has ever admired me before. We don't let ourselves, do we? I know what you admired me for – my umph! Just think, now I'm a stupid discarded old bag!

Who'd think they'd take a girl like me from the Woolwich Arsenal? But I was a looker. They needed me for my typing and to drop me into occupied territory with sovereigns and the codes for our agents. So many lovely young men and women going to who-knew-what in the scrum of war. All those ships in the night – I feel so ashamed! My hair wasn't dyed then –

it isn't dyed now, mind you – and everyone called me Ginger. Imagine if I'd been picked up – with my colouring and me speaking only une peu of French! But then, everyone was expendable although we didn't know it until later, we were so brainwashed with the Union Jack (la la la!) and bromide in the tea. I won't lift a finger for this war. Fancy, that we should see it all happen again.

That nurse, Gabriel, the one like a bull in kirby grips, said 'Lily, I've never seen anyone put up such a fight, she should have died ten days ago.' I love that girl. It's a lesson to me because I don't usually like plain people. There's nothing to hang on for. Old age has got no compensations. I put my foundation on and pull my glamour face then I get foundation in the tramlines! I suppose you've got her. She's with you now, isn't she?

That kills me. When you're her age, you think it won't happen to you. Then one day, you look in the mirror, and you feel sick. It's nothing you've eaten, nothing you've done. It's age staring back at you. Mind you, even though she is much younger than us, I've noticed her face slips towards night. That's why you cut me off so completely after the operation, isn't it? Because you couldn't bear the death in me and wanted a bit of innocence. But I know you still love me even if you've forgotten it. I can feel it around me, now more than ever. And I want you to listen very hard to what I'm writing.

It's going to be tonight, Jean. It's for the best. I've made my peace on that. And this is for us, this time, like a baby being born. Oh dear, I've slopped retz all down my front. I'm such a messy eater. My bosom catches everything. I've got that brochure with all the photographs. The Seven Days Cruise one in the Greek Islands. It's from before. Before, when we were together. Remember staggering into the travel agents to get it after knocking a few back down the pub. You know, that time you wrote your will on a couple of beer mats, and got some old crony to witness it and

150

you said 'Ginger, I leave you everything I have in the world. I couldn't love you more if you were God!' and you kissed me right there and then at lunchtime and I said 'I'm yours'. It's open in front of me. Not that we'd ever have afforded it, but it departs Pireus 18.00 on the Sunday, and there's the picture. And we're there.

Oh, I love Pireus. The feeling of life. The lights of the port and the *pousty* boys all dressed up as whores in their high heels and see-through blouses. I love it. Nothing's changed. All piggedly-higgedly. How well I know Pireus. See that ship up on the left – it must have been rusting there since the war. I've probably been on that ship. I can't think when I was last here. It must have been the Siege of Athens, the Civil war, you know. I remember a broken-down hotel up that street – the Blue House, that's what it was called – up there on the right or was it over there? – and meeting up with someone from the embassy for coffee and an affair. She'd got scared because of the soldiers and the tanks, and had packed up her curtains and three bags of sugar in a hold-all and was sitting on them, like a lemon! *Ya sou, Pireus!*

Heraklion on the Monday. That's the one with the Palace of Colossal. Something to do with a bull in a maze. Then Santori – Santorini – that's the black wiggly one, isn't it, with the volcano, that interupted quite recently?

This retzina stuff doesn't have any effect on me. I'm going to take half a Halcyon as a treat when it's all over, and sleep like a baby, like the dead. I had a terrible – it's the boulb boulb boulb of the merciless traffic – terrible night last night – that kept me awake.

I got the same words over and over again: 'da overshadow kelp na, da overshadow kelp na' along with the boulb boulb boulb. Kelp. That's a health food or should be. Kelpna. It was a telepathy something. Then the penny dawned. The boulb boulb boulb was you leaving, and then when I rang the hospital, they said it would be soon.

And here's Patmos of the Revelations where someone sat in a cave and wrote bits of the Bible. It's a steep hill. You might have to go up there on your own. We've had our up and downs, so many ups and downs, and we'll come through this one, you'll see.

Jean! You're drifting, drifting in yourself. I want you to concentrate. It's Ginger. You've got to let go, darling. I'm not frightened of dying because I don't believe in God and neither should you. Here's Delos. It'll be Wednesday now. No one's allowed to be born or to die on this island even today, it says, because of Appollo being born there. There's a single palmtree – it must be spring because it's girt with poppies – mind, but you've got to watch out for snakes, they can bite you through your socks – and that's what Leto held on to when she gave birth to him. And Leto's the name of our ship too which is resting in the turquoise port with its fairy lights switched off. It's hot. Mosquitoes, the smell of thyme. You can see the marble fallen in the water and all those ruins and you and me! And we've got to say goodbye. Jean, Jean, there's that blue blue sea. You slip into it. I'm going to miss you so much, don't think I'm not, it's tearing me up, but you do it! you show them! Die and do it where you're not meant to. I want you to call me 'Ginger' again. I want you to call me that so much. But you'll be all right, it's going to be all right.

I must have sizzed off. There's a great whirring noise in the room, like engines which woke me up. I'm not frightened. I can feel your hand in mine. Poor hands. Dying's such an energetic thing. Yes, yes, I can hear you. If this is all it is, it's not much. The worst's behind you now. That's it. You're doing it. Jean! Feel you. You've filled the whole room! You've knocked the breath out of my body. Here's to you. Stinny ya mas – down to the last drop.

PS. Friday. The hospital rang this morning. You died at exactly the time I felt you. Our magic is still there, isn't it, in spite of all the wrongs we've done each other? Then I got very angry, at having to do it on my own, and not being with you, not being allowed to see you, even one last time, or kiss you. Family and close relations only.

I was beside myself so I went out. I didn't know how I was going to cross the road. I pushed on a bus and went into a pub for a sandwich and a cider. Cider's much stronger than whiskey. I went to see Barbra Striesand in 'Mud' to cheer myself up. There wasn't a song in it. All set in a women's prison. 'Mud', or was it called 'Nuts'. 'Nuts', that's it. I knew it was a three lettered word. Then I waited for the bus home by the Social Security Towers. The times I've wanted to commit suicide there. The concrete. The grey. Desolate. Everyone does and there was a bomb, or another fire on the underground. But God's a strange thing. He moves in mysterious ways. There I was in the milling scrum when I heard a voice saying 'Hello, Lily,' and I felt this hand, and I turned round and it was my mate, Patty, from Weaving. And she said to me 'How are you?' and I said 'I've got some rotten news,' and she said 'what's the matter?' and I said 'It's Jean.' And she said 'Your partner?' and that broke me up. And I cried and I cried. She said she was worried about me and I said 'God's good to me. I needed to see you and he sent you.' She couldn't stop though. She was on her way to her uncle's funeral! You've got to laugh, haven't you? Any port in a storm, eh, Jean? Any port in a storm.

PPS. Wednesday. That vicar never even said your name. You wouldn't have known you were a woman. You'd have thought he wanted to rub it in that you weren't here. Fancied himself because he looked like a young Laurence of Oliver. Then she came up to me after the service and kissed me. She told me how much she loved you – just because I'm old enough to be her mother, she thinks I'm not jealous – and she shed a few tears. She was wearing the gold knot ring I gave you in Portsmouth on her wedding finger. I wanted to rip her eyes out. But I didn't. You'd have been proud of me.

153

I'm sending this care of Delos, Greece. That'll fox them. Be there when I arrive. I'm on the small boat being ferried across and I can see you standing in the shade of the tourist pavilion, waving and smiling, our pasts forgiven.

Until then. I miss you.
Love,
Ginger

*This story had its origins in *Mortal*, a play by Maro Green and Caroline Griffin.

AFTERWORD

J. E. Hardy

Patricia Duncker, the editor of *In and Out of Time*, wrote in her Afterword that 'Words change women's minds, change women's worlds'. I share this view. I believe in it strongly, and this belief no doubt shaped my editorial priorities.

Foucault wrote that 'The right to remain silent does not eliminate the need to speak.' I might go further and say that the need to speak does not eliminate the need to speak as well as one is able. When what has to be said is fundamentally at odds with the *status quo*, and challenges the very foundations of the established order, then the need to speak clearly becomes the need to speak beautifully. For words do indeed change minds and lives.

Lesbians do not live in a vacuum; the majority perforce live very much in the patriarchal world. We try to change that world, try to chip away at its constraints, prejudices, ignorance, violence. Yet our developing philosophies, ideologies, credos are often stymied by the scandals of defective, distorted reportage.

But there is always the word, the tool to subvert violence, to create anew.

In *The Pied Piper*, the editors described Clause 28 as 'a response to feminist gains and an explicit reference to the lesbians who achieved them'. In the space of five years, since the publication of *The Reach* in 1984, the climate in which we were writing had changed; the challenges and threats from the state and all its august bodies had become more apparent. In *The Pied Piper* the editors also said that the changes set in motion in the 1960s and 1970s had 'receded and were being fought for again within a very short time'. And those changes are being fought for again now, in the face of ever self-renewing prejudices, the burgeoning of neo-fascism, persecution in the name of the free-market, the seemingly unbreakable strangle-hold of the right on the throat of politics world-wide. And everywhere commentators refer to 'post-feminist times'. *Post*-feminist? It is as if we are expected to believe that the dreams of the 1960s and 1970s were just that – dreams. Unattainable, born out of a desire to be that which we cannot be. Here is the power of the word: repeat 'post-feminism' often enough, and the listener/ reader might well believe we are living in post-feminist times; that what we have is as much as we will get. Yet we can fire the establishment's boomerang bullet straight back. Repeat over and over those things you believe, those things that you know – and the word will spread.

And this brings me back to what I wrote earlier. Words are one of the tools we can use to try to change the world, try to change our lives. Lesbian-feminist novels, short stories, books of poetry, academic tracts, theoretical analyses are weapons of change. The concerns, the focus of these publications is always shifting, responding to the world and its threats and to new potentials.

I believe that lesbian-feminist writing has improved with each pssing year, as lesbians become more accomplished as writers, as we practise the craft, as more lesbians choose writing as a means of speaking to the world, as we discover the limitless possibilities of the word. We have to write stories and poems of ever-increasing clarity and quality for them to be read, for them to bring about change. One of the inspiring aspects of editing this collection was reading so many beautifully crafted stories by new writers.

Lesbian writing is an enduring weapon, the most insidious of all means of transformation, the least limited of resources. The more effectively it is used, the more effective it will be.

So, in a nutshell, that was my governing editorial policy – that what is written is written beautifully, is written well, is written in such a way that the reader is transported into the text, to find there her own concerns, or to be shown another's. That each story deconstructs the meanings of the world we live in, and finds within it other meanings. That each story blows wide open the doors of the mind and lets in Possibility.

CONTRIBUTORS' NOTES

Amanda Hayman: All Amanda Hayman's best stories contain an element of magic. She believes that Lesbians have untapped powers that could be invaluable in the overthrow of the patriarchy. Ten years into her Tokyo life, she revels in the joys of living alone, whilst continuing her relationship with her lover of ten years, who now lives down the road. A white, middle-class separatist, Amanda has had four or five short stories published, and is working on a novel about dykes and magic in Anglesey.

Aspen: I am a woman / I have a soft body / I have quite a few scars / I have not always had enough moisture to blossom forth / The challenge is living / life positive / insolent defiance / greatly daring / moving concrete slowly or with a sudden burst / the flowers in the crazy, crazy paving / can catch you napping / and take your breath away.

Unexpected gifts settle like grace / the warmth of love / mellows anguish / whatever the prevailing wind.

Caroline Natzler: Writing used to be some sort of compensation — for bordedom, loneliness, frustration — but now I cannot imagine life feeling replete without it. I teach writing at the City University and at Goldsmiths (both London). Despite being a Writer I do not divide my time between London and the South of France. I work four days a week as a local authority solicitor.

My book, *Water Wings* (Onlywomen Press), was published in 1990.

I also have stories in *The Reach* and *The Pied Piper* (Onlywomen Press), *Everyday Matters 11* (Sheba), and *Girls Next Door* (The Women's Press).

Cherry Potts: I live in South London with my lover and two cats, which makes me very happy. I work in local government, which drives me crazy. I am not as

i

old as I feel most of the time, but expect to catch up some time soon. Story-telling is a family tradition.

Helen Smith: Helen Smith was born in London in 1954. She has been writing short stories since the early 80s and has had a few published. She is one of the Outlanders, the Manchester-based lesbian writers' group. Her childhood ambition to read every book in the world has given way to wanting to complete writing one.

Hilary Bichovsky: I have not had a job for the past 11 years. During this time I have been to University, signed on, worked for Rape-Crisis, been a freelance journalist, exhibited my sculptures, performed my writing, sung my songs and last but not least (believe me) begun to grow a beard.

I am presently more hopeful about life than I have ever been. I am into healing, yoga, meditation, honesty, anger, health-giving food, counselling, affirmations, therapy ... the lot. In September I begin training in creative therapy.

I believe the world is capable of the complete transformation necessary to recover from the abuse of men. At any rate, I know I am, and that's a start.

Jaq Bayles: Jaq Bayles was born in London just as the sixties began to swing. Educated in Kent, she qualified as a journalist and propped her feet on many a newsdesk around the country before finally settling in Brighton – her spiritual home and most enduring love. She now shares a garden flat with a cat called Opus and assorted feline visitors. 'Skin Deep' is Jaq's second successful foray into short story writing, but The Novel is still underway. Other ventures have included stage plays and TV comedy scripts. Outside of writing she is an aspiring weekend club DJ and sometime bodybuilder.

J. E. Hardy: J. E. Hardy lives in Bristol, where she admires architecture, smokes too much and wonders at the inadequacies of the world. She hopes always that the world will change, will become what it could be but doubts this will happen. She hopes also that women will indeed see the possibilities that exist everywhere. If this collection enables them to do that just a little more often, she will have achieved what she intended.

Kym Martindale: Kym lives in Bristol with her lover, Sarah, and her cat, Hecate. They have a tiny house and work for the NHS and like to spend weekends in Shropshire. If they're not in Shropshire they enjoy breakfast at an excellent coffee house in Bristol on Saturday and go for walks on Sunday, that is if Kym isn't away drinking with an Irishman called Alistair who also teaches her tunes on the tin whistle.

Lis Whitelaw: Lis Whitlaw is the author of a biography of Cicely Hamilton, *The Life and Rebellious Times of Cicely Hamilton* (The Women's Press, 1990) and has also published short stories and various non-fiction pieces, includine one on lesbians in cinema, in *Gossip* 5. She has recently moved to Herefordshire where she is writing a novel, teaching creative writing and working in adult education.

Lucy Kimbell: Born 1966, white, of part-Irish descent and brought up in the south of England. I have since travelled and worked in various places including Sudan, the Gaza Strip, and Barcelona, where I worked on the Fourth International Feminist Bookfair and where I turned into a lipstick lesbian. I am currently working on a travel book about Poland, focusing on a pilgrimage to Our Lady of Czestochwe. I am also interested in women's theatre and 'experimental' performances. I would like to learn to weld properly. At present I live in Bristol, but who knows what next?

Maírín de Barra: Maírín was born sixth child of a seventh child, in a family of mystics across the water. She is sure some previous child got lost along the way. Her own seven have yet to be born. Meanwhile, a worker, she labours in other ways, as is the sad, historic fate of the Gael, awaiting the day that Celts rediscover each other. In her spare time she cuts other people's grass, forgets to become accustomed to renting a video, and pretends that the wind in the trees is really the sea.

Maro Green: Born 1948, trained as a dancer and then as an actress. Has worked in theatre since 1968. As Penny Casdagli she is the Artistic Co-Director of the Neti-Neti Theatre Company which publishes and performs plays for young people in English, Sign Language and Bengali, and as Maro Green she is author of several short stories published by Onlywomen Press and the The Women's Press, and co-author of such plays as *More* (Gay Sweatshop), *The Memorial Gardens* (Nitty Gritty Theatre Company) and *Mortal* (The Women's Theatre Group).

Onlywomen Press publishes fiction, theory and poetry by lesbians to express and illuminate a developing Radical Feminism. Our 'Liaison' list titles are part of a programme to overtly encourage Lesbian Feminist Studies. Any of these may be purchased by mail-order directly from Onlywomen or from any good bookshop.

For a free catalogue detailing all our titles and information about our trade distributors both in the U.K. and abroad send S.A.E. to:
ONLYWOMEN PRESS, 38 Mount Pleasant, London WC1X 0AP, U.K.

THEORY

LESBIAN TEXTS AND CONTEXTS: Radical Revisions *U.K. only*
edited by Karla Jay & Joanne Glasgow

Anthology of literary criticism. (416 pages)
"The first collection of exclusively lesbian criticism ever published ... intelligent, arousing, a little stubborn about what it means, in semiotics and material terms, to be a lesbian".
ISBN 0–906500–40–0

FOR LESBIANS ONLY: a separatist anthology
edited by Sarah Lucia-Hoagland & Julia Penelope

The world's first anthology of lesbian separatism. (608 pages) Documents twenty years of activism and scholarship. *"defined not by rejection of the male-dominated world but by the committment of one's best energy to lesbians." "something to cut through ... post-feminist confusion like a hot knife through butter".*
ISBN 0–906500–28–1

WOMEN AGAINST VIOLENCE AGAINST WOMEN
edited by Sandra McNeill and dusty rhodes

Three sets of conference papers discussing pornography, rape and feminist action. "exposes some of feminism's simplest, cleverest, most effective politics".
ISBN 0–906500–16–8

THE SAFE SEA OF WOMEN: Lesbian Fiction 1969–89

U.K. only

Bonnie Zimmerman

Literary criticism. "the definitive analysis of lesbian fiction for some years to come ... describes major themes, changes and transitions in the growth of feminist-era lesbian literature."
ISBN 0–906500–42–7

POETRY

THE HANG-GLIDER'S DAUGHTER: new and selected poems
Marilyn Hacker

"Elegant and versatile in the strictest forms, she is inventive and exuberant in content ... colloquial, lyrical, uncouth, old fashioned and fun." "intimate and intellectual at the same time."
ISBN 0–906500–36–2

BECAUSE OF INDIA: selected poems and fables
Suniti Namjoshi

"blending that which is uncompromisingly Indian in her with the best of the English satirical tradition." "intelligent and passionate, skilful but never slick".
ISBN 0–906500–33–8

PASSION IS EVERYWHERE APPROPRIATE
Caroline Griffin

"a kind of mysticism which, howevever, is always earthed in the experience of lesbian feminism."
ISBN 0–906500–34–6

BEAUTIFUL BARBARIANS: lesbian feminist poetry
edited by Lilian Mohin

A selective anthology; 16 poets. *"often make clear the points at which they intersect with mainstream tradition ..." "the tough wisdom of exiles and the poignant idealism of expatriates".*
ISBN 0–906500–23–0

THE WORK OF A COMMON WOMAN   *U.K. only*
(poems 1964–77)
Judy Grahn

Poetry from the heart of the Women's Liberation Movement.
"what the movement used to feel like a lot of the time, and reading it you start to believe it still can."
ISBN 0–906500–20–6

ONE FOOT ON THE MOUNTAIN: British Feminist Poetry
1969–79
edited by Lilian Mohin

55 poets with photos and biographical notes.
"does give pleasure, but is neither soothing nor calming: it is altogether more intense and vital."
ISBN 0–906500–01–X

LOVE, DEATH AND THE CHANGING OF THE SEASONS
                                              U.K. only
Marilyn Hacker

Sonnets that make a novel: about a tempestuous love affair.
"wholly modern in tone and language, its author's batteries are charged with the tradition of Shakespeare, Blake, Yeats and Pound."
ISBN 0–906500–26–5

FICTION

HATCHING STONES
Anna Wilson

A mordantly witty novel set in the near future when easy, successful cloning forces a re-examination of the issues of gender and male supremacy.
ISBN 0–906500–39–7

STEALING TIME
Nicky Edwards

A novel set in the last years of the twentieth century, with a rascally 14 year old at its centre initiating corporate fraud to improve the lives of urban women.
ISBN 0–906500–31–1

CACTUS
Anna Wilson
A realistic novel exploring the lives of two lesbian couples: *"one modern ... one which broke up some twenty years before, mostly through social pressures ... a clear and gentle tone."*
ISBN 0–906500–04–4

ALTOGETHER ELSEWHERE
Anna Wilson
A novel about women as vigilantes, varied in race, class and sexuality; united only in desperation. *"always humming with energy"*. *"a book with an afterlife – sinister and playful"*.
ISBN 0–906500–18–4

RELATIVELY NORMA
Anna Livia
A very humorous novel set (mostly) in Australia where a London lesbian feminist 'comes out' to her family. *"fast, furious and teeters on the knife-edge of feminist farce"*.
ISBN 0–906500–10–9

BULLDOZER RISING
Anna Livia

A science fiction novel written with bone chilling glee about a 'secret congress' of old women who plot survival. *"exemplary, brilliantly written satire ... completely invigorating"*.
ISBN 0–906500–27–3

STRANGER THAN FISH
short stories
J. E. Hardy.
ISBN 0–906500–32–X

WATER WINGS
short stories
Caroline Natzler
ISBN 0–906500–38–9

A NOISE FROM THE WOODSHED
short stories
Mary Dorcey

Winner of the 1990 Rooney Prize for Irish Literature.
ISBN 0–906500–30–3

SACCHARIN CYANIDE   *U.K. only*
short stories
Anna Livia.
ISBN 0–906500–35–4

INCIDENTS INVOLVING WARMTH:
lesbian feminist love stories
Anna Livia.
ISBN 0–906500–21–4

THE NEEDLE ON FULL: lesbian feminist science fiction
short stories
Caroline Forbes.
ISBN 0–906500–19–2

IN AND OUT OF TIME: lesbian feminist fiction
short stories
edited by Patricia Duncker.

The 1990 anthology. 18 stories plus Patricia's introduction.
ISBN 0–906500–37–0

THE PIED PIPER: lesbian feminist fiction
short stories
edited by Anna Livia & Lilian Mohin

The 1989 anthology. 19 authors.
ISBN 0–906500–29–X

THE REACH: lesbian feminist fiction
short stories

edited by Lilian Mohin & Sheila Shulman
The first lesbian feminist anthology in Britain (1984).
ISBN 0–906500–15–X